LOVE BITES

LOVE BITES

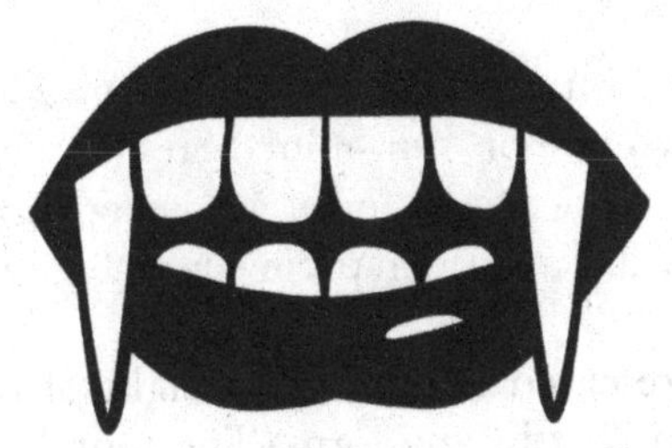

KYT WRIGHT

BLKDOG

www.blkdogpublishing.com

LOVE BITES

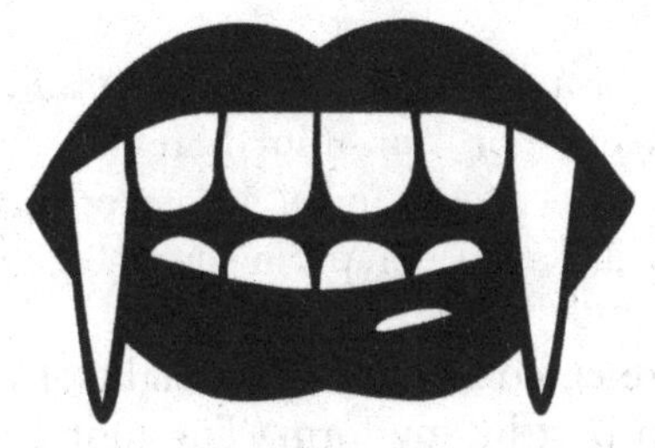

KYT WRIGHT

Copyright © 2019 Kyt Wright.

This edition published in 2019 by BLKDOG Publishing.

No part of this publication may be reproduced, stored in a retrieval system, or transmitted in any form or by any means, electronic, mechanical, photocopying, recording, or otherwise, without written permission of the publisher.

All rights reserved including the right of reproduction in whole or in part in any form. The moral right of the author has been asserted.

This is a work of fiction. Names, characters, businesses, places, events, locales, and incidents are either the products of the author's imagination or used in a fictitious manner. Any resemblance to actual persons, living or dead, or actual events is purely coincidental.

BLKDOG

www.blkdogpublishing.com

Chapter One – Petar

"Of course the undead can be killed in as many ways as the living, but the surest way is an iron spike through the heart and then decapitation."

Tina regarded the man sitting opposite her who appeared to be in his thirties, he was saturnine, dark-haired and handsome, a toothy smile being the only clue to his true nature. "So not a wooden stake then?" she asked.

"Oh a wooden stake will work but it is terribly inefficient, iron does something to our blood and renders the victim helpless," he replied. "Wood can also splinter on ribs and I am told that is very painful." The curtains in the dingy hotel room were tightly closed even though it was the darkest night outside, *it showed consideration* he thought.

"That's an interesting definition of victim Count Orlov." suggested Tina.

The man steepled his long fingers and shrugged. "It depends on which side of the fence you are sitting and please do call me Petar."

"I must say Petar you are being very open about your life sorry... unlife?" they had been talking for half an hour and the vampire had seemed quite eager to tell all."

"I do not worry, these things are easy to find in books and on the internet. All people have to do is read, something they don't seem to do nowadays, it is because of internet, it is very sad," he replied in his East-European accent.

"Well I hope they'll read my book Count Orlov, thank you for the interview it's been a real experience," opening her sports bag Tina put the I-pad away. "Best let you get away before cock-crow."

"I do not like to think of the cock's crow or the dawn," pausing, he looked at her meaningfully. "Ahem, my payment?" asked the Count.

"Oh sorry, I nearly forgot." Tina unbuttoned her blouse to bare her long neck. "It won't hurt will it?"

"It may smart a little at first, but it will soon pass, you know, you are a very pretty girl? Tina, is that short for something?"

"My name is Christiana, remember we agreed only a small amount?" she replied, nervously fingering her crucifix.

He held her in his gaze and bared long canines. "My apologies, I forgot to mention the cross does not work on us, also I forgot to mention you cannot trust a vampire around pretty girls, especially one as lovely as you. I am sure your blood will be as delightful to drink as your lips will be to ki..." Count Orlov stopped mid-sentence and looked down in astonishment at what was sticking in his chest.

"It's a wooden-handled iron spike, I make them myself," explained Tina driving it in further. "Sometimes you shouldn't trust a pretty girl around vampires."

Orlov stood there paralysed as she drew the cutlass from its scabbard in the sports bag and with well-practised ease lopped off his head in a single swing. Tina dragged the decapitated corpse, *corpse once more*, out onto the balcony, comfortable in the knowledge that the dawn sun would turn it to ash. Picking up the desiccated head, still with a look of surprise on its face, she took a photo of it with her phone as proof then popped it into a canvas bag for later incineration. The photo she would send to a certain department in the Vatican who would log it and send her payment by return. Her next excision was in Antwerp then she could return home for a while. *"Well, after going to all that trouble I didn't learn anything new!"* thought Christiana Van Helsing as she finished packing away. *"Still, there's always next time."*

After turning out the light, she closed the door quietly and left.

CHAPTER TWO - HARKER

A dark foggy night found Constable James Harker examining the body of a young man slumped awkwardly against a wall in the alley behind the Green Goblin, the landlord had found the body while taking out a crate of empties and the young policeman was the first responder.

"His throats a right mess!" observed the landlord unhelpfully.

That's an understatement! Thought Harker holding back from retching, the man's throat looked as if had been torn open by an animal. "They look like teeth marks." he mused aloud, oddly there was hardly any blood.

"Ruddy hell I'm not staying out here, if you want anything I'll be inside!" with that the publican shut the side door and the policeman heard the lock click.

Harker could get no signal, *where was his backup, where were forensics?* The fog rolled towards him like a special effect from a nineteen sixties horror film and sending out misty tendrils as if probing for him. With the publican now locked safely behind his strong door, Harker felt uncom-

fortably alone, the constable's first night shift had got off to a particularly inauspicious start and now to make things worse the sound of approaching footsteps was echoing eerily through the gloom.

Nerves on edge Harker shone his torch towards the sound and called out shakily. "Who's there?"

The footsteps stopped and he could make out the outline of a figure in the fog then a voice with an unusual accent rang out. "WPS Bathory, what's the problem here Constable?" the shape resolved itself into the figure of a woman and to his relief he saw she was wearing a police uniform.

"A dead body, throat all ripped out Sarge I've never seen anything like it before, didn't you hear it on the radio?"

"No, the bugger's playing up, you can't pick up much down here, something to do with the stonework," she replied.

Harker, new to the station had never seen this officer before and he would have certainly remembered if he had, she was possibly in her forties with an attractive fine-boned face with pale skin with ash blonde, almost white hair and she was sporting bright red lip gloss. *The Inspector would surely have something to say about that!*

"Are you from Bishopgate then Sarge?" he asked curiously, her hatband wasn't the red and white check of the City Police.

"I have a mobile assignment, I move between stations," she explained then peering past him asked. "Well Constable, can I see this body?"

"Yeah I suppose so." he was puzzled by this strange officer and her old fashioned uniform. *When was the last time a policewoman wore a skirt on duty?*

The sergeant knelt to examine the wound at close range. "This is not good, not good at all, the culprit must be found."

"That's our job isn't it?" began Harker but the sergeant cut him off with a glare.

"Someone is going to pay dearly for this, we're not supposed to kill, just take what we need!" she sniffed at the air then dipped a long finger into the wound and licked at the blood seeming to relish it. "Quite fresh, not been dead too long."

"What the..?" exclaimed Harker in shock, *had he really just seen that?*

Sgt Bathory stood and walked towards the helpless constable, now transfixed by her deep brown eyes. "Sorry Constable, I couldn't resist it, rather let the cat out of the bag didn't I?" she grabbed his shoulders. "This won't hurt and you won't remember anything, but I promise I'll get whoever did this."

Harker stood feeling confused and rubbing his neck, he could make out several figures approaching through the mist. "Hello... hello?" he called, *had something just happened?*

"Go on Harker say it again and make my night." it was Sergeant Gillman from Bishopsgate station with another officer. "SOCO's coming up behind us, sorry we're late there was a sodding accident at the junction," he looked at the body. "Bloody hell that's nasty!" he regarded the constable's grey face. "This is your first death isn't it Harker?"

"Yeah Sarge." he pulled a face.

"That's not the victim's blood on your collar is it?" asked the sergeant curiously.

Harker carefully felt his neck to find two small nicks a short distance apart, they were beginning to itch. "I must have cut myself shaving?" he couldn't remember when.

CHAPTER THREE – CHRISTIANA

Christiana Van Helsing stood at the tall rectangular window of her home that looked out over the canal, it was a sunny day, residents and tourists alike bustled below on foot or bicycle. She had trapped her last victim in Bruges, torturing it with garlic oil and bursts of UV light, finally getting some useful information before finishing it with spike and sword. *"Victim?"* she thought. *"Curse you Count Olav!"* she had never thought as them as such before, now it played on her mind.

Her venerable precedents had believed that *excising* vampires in the correct manner would release their souls allowing them to go to heaven, Tina believed that was all crap, to her they were little more than bloodthirsty psychopaths with the ability to spread their affliction to others. They rarely created new vampires for fear it would upset what they considered the natural order and kept the killing to a minimum for fear of alerting their cattle, humanity, of their existence. They did have their obedient servants however from whom they would occasionally take blood to keep under their thrall, worse still, some humans were willing to become their playthings or pets.

***

Amsterdam, like most tourist cities, had at least one of the creatures *unliving* here taking its pick from the steady flow of visitors, the idea of a *Nosferatu* at large in her home town made her blood boil but thanks to her last excision Tina knew where to look for the creature.

Grigori left the Red Light Bar to observe the throng of humans in search of after-hours and possibly illicit entertainment, which the Wallen provided in spades, the red-light district was one of his favourite haunts and offered rich pickings to a predatory soul. A group of young women giggled their way by and he briefly considered following to separate one from the herd as it were. He restrained himself, feeling he needed a change *and anyway they were probably stoned or drunk or both*, vampires were affected by narcotics and alcohol in much the same way their food source and since rumours were circulating about a spiker operating in the Low Countries, felt he ought to keep a clear head for safety's sake. Grigori generally left the window sitters well alone too for other blood-related concerns. With the aroma of garlic issuing from a nearby pizza restaurant making him uneasy he crossed the road to give it a wide berth bumping into a young man as he did.

"Oh I'm sorry, please do forgive me sir!" said the effete youth.

Grigori looked him over, the lad was tall fair and handsome with finely plucked eyebrows, he was well turned out and wearing powerful cologne, *he would do!* "Not at all, it was my fault entirely!" he replied with a grin, his sharp canines not as yet extended. "My name's Grigori, how come I've not seen you around here before?"

"New to the district, I'm Pieter, would you be looking for some company?" asked the youth with a nervous smile.

"I might be." Replied Grigori, the guy was obviously

a prostitute. "You're not sat in a window, isn't that a tiny bit illegal in De Walletjes?" the youth appeared to be fit and healthy, it occurred to him that he hadn't drained a human for a while. The thought was very tempting.

"Only if they catch you handsome?" he raised his well-maintained brows. "I have a place just around the corner."

Grigori grinned again. "Lead the way, young man," eagerly following the rent-boy into an alleyway, he had already extended his fangs when something hard and heavy hit him on the head.

"Bloody hell you must have killed him!" exclaimed Pieter in horror, staring at the wound inflicted on the vampire's skull.

"No, I just stunned the bastard, but it will take a while to heal," replied Tina hefting the studded mace and checking that Grigori was genuinely out for the count.

Pieter helped her tie the unconscious vampire with garlic impregnated rope and together they dragged him into a dark cellar nearby. "Is this the one that killed Ambroos?"

"More than likely," she replied, the aforementioned Ambroos had been her neighbour and the love of Pieter's life before being found floating in the canal, the verdict had been death from exsanguination.

"You are going to deal with the bastard properly aren't you?" he asked looking at the red blisters forming around the vampire's bound wrists. "Do you need any help?"

"No thank you Piet, you've done more than enough already and you really don't want to be around when I start working on the creature but you can rest assured it's days of preying on humans are over!" after refusing the money she tried to press into his palm, Pieter left Christiana alone with Grigori.

Opening her large sports bag, she laid out various vials and implements on the table and checked the batteries in her UV lamp. The vampire began to stir, so keeping her finger over the lamp's switch she squatted down next to him. He began to moan at the garlic-infused rope burning his skin. "Nice to have you back with us Grigori Ilyich, now I have a few questions for you."

Chapter Four – Liz

Sgt Bathory knocked on the door of the first floor flat and looked nervously at the lightening sky. *The sun would be up shortly!*

The door opened a crack and a voice came from behind. "Who is it?"

"Police!" she replied.

"Oh, I'd better let you in." the chain was unfastened and the door opened to allow Bathory through, the occupant was a well-proportioned young Goth woman with long jet black hair in a leather Basque and fishnets.

"Unusual nightwear if I might be so bold, madam?" suggested Bathory.

The girl shrugged. "Has there been a crime committed sergeant?"

"There might well have been, I'm afraid I'm going to have to ask you some questions."

"Will you have to search me?" asked the young woman coyly.

"Almost certainly madam," replied the sergeant.

"The girl held her arms outstretched. "Will it be a strip search?"

"I'm afraid so madam, but you can leave the stockings

on," they shared a passionate kiss. "Of course I'm going to have to take my clothes off too."

Liz Stride, looked at Beth's lithe form on the bed, her lover was centuries-old but appeared to only be in her forties, with pale almost translucent skin and as counterpoint possessed sensuous full red lips and eyes of the deepest brown. They had met at a Goth bar in Soho and feeling mutual attraction hit it off immediately and laughed at the fact they were called Elizabeth and Elisabeth. After agreeing they should be Liz and Beth the pale woman had asked her if she'd ever met a real vampire before, Liz had considered it an off the wall chat up line but after a drink or five they had gone to a quiet alley *to be alone*. Bathory rather intoxicated, had unsuccessfully tried to transfix Liz with her brown eyes while extending her fangs to bite, to the vampire's surprise the girl did not struggle but instead bared her neck to find the experience strangely arousing. Elizabeth Stride worked in the A&E at The Royal London Hospital and found her shift hours quite conducive to having a relationship with a *creature of the night* as Beth sometimes referred to herself. Liz knew her lover worked as a police officer with a special dispensation who reported to somebody very high up in Whitehall, but she rarely discussed her work, occasionally seeming distracted, *was there a special police force for vampires?*

Beth gave her a sweet but guilty smile, Liz knew the look. "Are you hungry?"

"Would you mind?"

Liz climbed back on the bed for Beth to cradle her, brushing her long black hair aside she caressed the side of her neck with her lips then sealing them upon it pushed the tips of her extended canines into the woman's jugular, swallowing the warm blood as it squirted into her mouth. When Beth estimated she'd taken half a pint she withdrew her fangs and keeping her lips fastened tightly cleaned up the blood with her tongue, disinfecting it with her saliva as the two small punctures closed. "You okay?"

Liz gazed into her eyes. "Mmm, it always makes me a little woozy and a lot horny."

Beth licked her lips clean. "Then I'd better see what I can do about that…"

CHAPTER FIVE – REMEMBRANCE

The three figures carried their wreaths to the grave in the pouring rain, written on the stone cross were the birth and death dates of the deceased along with two short sentences. The first stated simply, *Markus Van Helsing, loving husband and brave father,* while below, the other read, *Ilse Van Helsing, much missed and beloved mother, a life so unfairly taken.* A framed photograph portrayed the couple in happier times.

Eleven years ago, revered *spiker* Markus Van Helsing had been outsmarted while tracking down one of the *elders,* the creature had captured first Marcus then his wife, forcing him to watch while it tortured and then turned her. After the new vampiress had eagerly fed upon her husband she was sent to kill the teenage Christiana and her younger siblings, Erik and Fleur. The apprentice spiker had been left with no choice but to perform her first excision upon her own mother.

Markus Van Helsing had been buried with the urn containing Ilse's sun-burned ashes in his hands then leaving her brother and sister in the care of their since-deceased grandparents (both from natural causes), Christiana had set off on her unending crusade to destroy every vampire she could find.

The creature that had so cruelly treated her parents had eluded her thus far but under considerable duress her latest catch Grigori, believing her promise to spare him, had told her of a nosferatu across the Engelse Kanaal who knew the old one's identity. Christiana, of course, had no intention of sparing the creature but did excise it quickly and mercifully as recompense.

The Van Helsing children laid their wreaths on the grave, joined hands and each looked in the other's teary eyes, Fleur was now a well-known actress while Erik, a brigadier in the police constantly on the alert for suspicious blood-related murders. All three siblings carried a vial of concentrated garlic oil at all times and each possessed an interesting collection of pointed and sharp-edged tools.

Christiana hugged them and after being admonished to take care, left the pair to walk alone towards the cemetery gate. She had travelled all across Europe in her campaign but had never visited England before, let alone London. The creature she sought inhabited the White-chapel area and she knew of a group who could help her find it.

***

The lovers had got up well after midday and Elisabeth sat riveted to the news channel while Liz busied herself getting ready for work, pulling back the curtain slightly to see what the weather was doing she remarked. "It's nice outside."

"*Bassza,* shut that unless you want to see me catch fire!" shouted Beth hiding her face behind a cushion.

"Is sunlight really that bad?" asked the nurse.

"It's not the light it's the UV, it would fry my skin like bacon, enough exposure and I would burn to ash, it's a horrible way to end your existence."

"Doesn't glass stop UV?"

"Everything at UVB and above but not UVA, the jury is out whether that's dangerous to the undead and I'm in no rush to find out, so keep those bloody curtains closed!" her interest was drawn back to the TV which was reporting the discovery of the body in the alleyway, a police statement followed stating they had no leads yet but were studying CCTV footage from the area.

"Is that where you were last night?" Liz on seeing her lover's attention decided to hazard a guess.

"Yes, it wasn't pleasant."

"Was it a vampire?" she asked.

"Almost certainly," replied Beth. "Looked like blood rage."

"Yuck, nothing will show up on the CCTV though, will it?"

"What?"

"Well you lot don't show up on cameras do you, you know like the mirror thing?"

"I have a reflection don't I?" she replied in exasperation. "Liz, you really mustn't believe everything you see in horror films."

"Will it kill again?"

"I imagine so, once you get a taste for killing it's hard to stop," she replied sadly and Liz held her for a while. "You're not still using that rucksack?" she asked upon spotting the bag on the nurse's shoulders. It was pink and had unicorns all over it, she had bought it for Liz after she had joked that if vampires were real unicorns might be, Bathory, had laughingly replied that in all her years of undeath she had never seen one.

"Of course Beth, I treasure everything you give me!" she replied breezily before going off to the hospital.

Bathory's mobile rang, the caller id simply read "D" she had been expecting this.

"Ah, Elisabeth I hope I haven't disturbed you." said a cultured voice.

"No John, I was already awake," she replied. "This is about last night isn't it?"

"Yes, the Executive has organised an emergency meeting in Whitehall at 10 pm."

"Everyone?" *some of them would have to come from as far as Scotland in vehicles with blacked-out windows.*

"Everyone, so make sure you're there!"

CHAPTER SIX - BATHORY

PC James Harker signed in at the Bishopsgate police station hoping tonight's shift would be less traumatic. Two weeks ago he had transferred down from Nottingham full of enthusiasm to be part of the City police but until yesterday it had been one long round of directing tourists, recording petty theft plus the occasional fight.

He had slept uneasily during the day, a haunting image plaguing his dreams. He was back in the foggy alley where a policewoman was biting the throat of a man up against the wall, his dead eyes staring accusingly at him. The woman noticing his presence turned her face up, her mouth dripping blood then left her victim to stride menacingly towards him… He woke in a cold sweat and tried to remember what had happened… he had examined the body, called it in, had a brief conversation with the landlord and waited what seemed like an eternity for backup, *hadn't he?*

Putting it to the back of his mind he prepared to set off on his beat, Sgt Gillman was walking with him for a while tonight, the older policeman had recognised how shaken up his new charge was and decided to lend him some moral support. As they made to leave Harker heard a woman's voice in the Inspector's office.

"I have an urgent appointment to attend Inspector, but remember I am to be kept in the loop at all times." A WPS stood in the doorway, her accent was strange but somehow familiar.

He could not hear Singh's response clearly but he did not sound happy.

"I promise I will try not to tread on your toes, *too much*," she said in a more conciliatory tone and on leaving the office, escorted by the inspector, she glanced briefly at the two officers before strutting out on her non-regulation heels.

As Inspector Singh walked back to his office he turned his head towards the pair to mouth silently. "That bloody woman!"

Harker's heart skipped a beat it was the woman from his dream. "Who was that?"

"*Sergeant Batty*," whispered Gillman, admiring the seams on her stockings as she strode out.

"Huh?" asked the constable.

"Sergeant Bathory she is really, the lads call her the "Vampire" because she only seems to work the night shift, an odd fish, to say the least, gives me the right creeps sometimes. Doesn't give much of a shit about dress code and talks to the higher ranks like they're below her, you know this isn't even the bitch's manor yet she walks in and out like she owns the place?" Gillman shook his head and added conspiratorially. "Rumour has it Batty reports directly to Whitehall."

"That's a bit weird?"

"You're not kidding." agreed the sergeant.

Bathory, why does that name ring a bell? Harker mused as he walked the beat with Gillman. Apart from breaking up a fight between two drunks the night passed without incident and PC Harker retired gratefully to bed only to dream of the odd policewoman again, her face pressed up close to his while whispering something into his ear. After getting up in time for lunch he googled Bathory while eating a cheese sandwich and was surprised by the results. Elisabeth Bathory had been a Hungarian noblewoman born in the sixteenth century with a reputation for cruel and sadistic behaviour, often preying on her young maidservants yet capable of acts of incredible charity and benevolence, particularly towards wronged women. Some pundits said the reports were considerably exaggerated while others even claimed she was the victim of a plot to deprive the woman of her considerable wealth and property. Nonetheless, Elisabeth Bathory ended her days walled up in her chambers, dying after four and a half years a prisoner there. She'd had four children so it was possible the sergeant was descended from one of them, he studied various representations of the woman that ranged from a serious-looking young woman to a hawk-faced harridan and none seemed a likely candidate to be the mysterious sergeant's ancestor. Unsurprisingly the original version had earned the epithet the Blood Countess and even Countess Dracula with several sensational and gory films made about her.

Harker determined he would find out who this modern-day Bathory was.

***

Meanwhile, in a rented room, Christiana was practising her swing with the Polish cavalry sabre she had bought on the Portobello Road. The blade was longer than she would have liked but her desire to get to London quickly had meant she didn't have time to organise an import license for her favourite weapon, the replacement was well-balanced though and had polished and sharpened nicely. The bandolier of garlic *bombs* and tailor-made spikes, she had brought in her hold luggage, declaring openly that they were a vampire-killing kit destined for an art installation. The TV news was showing a report regarding the shocking discovery of a body behind a pub with a serious neck injury, Tina recognised the manner in which the victim had met his end, the crime might not have been committed by her quarry but it was certainly proof that at least one of the creatures was at large in London.

CHAPTER SEVEN –
EXECUTIVE

The Executive of Ten met in a panelled chamber within the depths of Whitehall, very few people knew who used the constantly locked room, the Freemasons being the "usual suspects" and while it was true a couple were here tonight, this gathering held greater import than any high powered lodge meeting. The Executive originally had consisted of thirteen vampyrs, one had been exiled for unrepentant sadomasochism towards humans and two more had met their end at the hands of spikers, the brethren's term for those who hunted their kind.

"Brothers and sisters, as you are no doubt aware a human was exsanguinated in Whitechapel last night, our sister Elisabeth in her role as Enforcer had a chance to examine the body at the crime scene and can confirm the man had been killed by one of us! This is in direct contravention of the edict that has stood us in good stead for over a hundred years, it is a serious matter and we must be on our guard as the killer may strike again soon, this rogue vampyr is probably still in London but may well have moved to an area under your auspices. I ask you to keep watch and ask your subjects if they know anything…"

Dee was interrupted by a stern *sire* with an impressive moustache, the newest member of the Executive who had been in the UK for only a century. "Is our sister certain it was one of our kind, I mean we all know how indulgent you are towards the cattle, isn't that right Erzsebet?"

She hadn't been called that for centuries but then Gyorgy Thurzo had good reason to remember her name. "I can assure you, *Georgie*, the victim's neck wounds clearly point to the murderer being a vampyr." there were several sharp intakes of breath.

"Victim, murderer?" snarled Thurzo, as angry at her using the Anglicized version of his name as he was at her choice of words. "Do not honour our food by using those terms, our brethren may be victims of murder but cattle are merely slaughtered! Just because you lower yourself to fornicate with them don't for one moment believe that they are our equal. Once we used to bleed humans dry whenever we desired and without remorse."

"You should be ashamed Georgie, we were all human once!" retorted Bathory.

"It is you who should be ashamed Erzsebet," said Thurzo looking at her accusingly. "I remember being human and I well remember who my *dam* was, *kibaszott leszbikus állat szar.*"

Bathory had no answer for his insult, she should call him out *but what point would it serve?*

Several of the Executive were whispering to each other as John Dee stood. "Brother Thurzo, our sister is held in the highest esteem and I demand that you apologize to her immediately."

"I will not, we have become weak and few while the cattle grow in strength and number, why bring the Executive together just to discuss one of our number giving in to natural instinct?"

"Brother Thurzo, I understand that recently arrived from the East you have a different outlook to your British brethren. We have maintained discretion for centuries and it has served us well, the humans now think of us as mere myth, stories which find credence only with certain people on the fringe like the Watcher group. We take what is necessary, no more and no-one is the wiser for it. Once this miscreant is caught, this *murder* will be remembered by the humans as the act of an unidentified psychopath. The balance must be maintained!"

Thurzo stood. "When the humans begin excising us en masse you might think differently and as for the Watchers, are they not always looking for a way to prove our existence? And do you know there is talk of a spiker heading to the city, one, who it is rumoured has almost singlehandedly eradicated our kind from the Low Countries?" he had their full attention now. "The Watchers almost certainly have something to do with it and what is more this spiker is rumoured to be one of Van Helsing's spawn." he finished his speech to a chorus of shocked gasps.

"What about Pulaski, he unlives over there and if that pervert had been excised I'm sure we'd have heard about that?" growled a vampire called McGregor who enforced the Edict in Scotland.

"As far as I know he is still with us" answered Thurzo.

"Of course, that bastard is your friend isn't he?" asked McGregor

"Pulaski does as his nature demands, I will not judge any of the brethren for that!" stated Thurzo.

"Can you prove that a Van Helsing excised all the vampyrs in Northern Europe, Georgie?" the Scot continued, unwilling to let it go.

"Can you conclusively prove that one of our kin *murdered* a food animal?" countered Thurzo.

"We were driven from the East because we did as our nature demanded, let us not forget that!" Elisabeth had found her voice again. "I fled, running by night and hiding by day until reaching this country where I was made welcome, it is not in our nature to change but the cattle, as some call them, do! They have developed weapons which had they possessed when they hunted us all those years ago, this conversation would not be happening because we would no longer exist!"

"Pah, further evidence of how weak we have become!" Thurzo snarled before striding from the room.

"So that went well!" opined McGregor.

As the Executive dispersed John walked with Elisabeth to the door of the building. "I'm worried about Thurzo, he was openly showing dissent," he remarked.

"Showing dissent? John he hijacked the meeting, I should have called him out for his insult."

"No Elisabeth, it does not suit for members of the Executive to fight each other and besides Thurzo has support from several others."

"So what do we do if more bodies turn up with their throats torn out? How long will it be before people start listening to the Watchers them instead of mocking them?" asked Bathory.

"That won't happen, Elisabeth, the British public are reserved by inclination and it'll take more than a few rabble-rousers to stir them into action."

"I hope you're right John, I remember having to flee for my unlife across Europe, what does your contact within the human government say of this?"

Dee appeared uncomfortable. "He is as yet not aware that an undead may be the culprit." he pursed his pale lips. "You must find this killer of humans, Elisabeth!"

CHAPTER EIGHT – PRYING

Harker was on desk duty tonight. He had tried in vain to find Bathory on the police computer and found nothing and it was almost as if she didn't exist. Hearing a cough he looked up guiltily to see the object of his fixation stood on the other side of the hatch, after being let in she gave him a pleasant smile then marched straight into the Inspector's office shutting the door behind her.

Jenny Jackson came in shortly after with PC Redmond in tow. "That bitch has got some front." remarked the WPC.

"Who?" asked Harker, *he had a good idea.*

"The "Vampire", she's just parked her bloody car on the double yellows outside the station!" she replied.

"So what she's a copper, like us?" *I think?*

"It's not a police car," said Redmond. "It's a bloody BMW Z3 hardtop, looks like the Batmobile!"

Harker knew he had to move quickly. "Jenny, hold the fort for a moment, I want to take a look at Batty's car!" leaving WPC Jackson on the desk he rushed outside and there it stood, shiny black and somehow menacing. Its windows so opaque it was a wonder anyone could see to drive, he quickly jotted down the registration number and rushed back just in time to take his seat as Bathory re-emerged from Singh's office.

She looked at him and smiled again. "Goodnight Constable Harker."

"Goodnight ma'am," he replied, shocked that she had spoken to him, shocked that she knew his name and even more shocked to see she had canine teeth that were notice-ably pointy, *perhaps she is a vampire?*

"Ooh, goodnight Constable Harker!" parroted Red-mond in a mocking voice when she had left. "Watch it, Jim, she's after you."

"She's more like a strippergram than a copper with those bloody heels and seamed stockings," muttered WPC Jackson.

"Sour grapes Jen?" remarked the constable. "We all know you fancy Jim yourself."

"Shut it Redmond!" she retorted, blushing visibly.

"Jenny?" asked in Harker in surprise. The WPC made an unintelligible comment and quickly left the front office followed by her grinning companion. As soon as he was alone Harker ran a PNC on the car to find it was reg-istered to a Miss Elizabeth Bathgate, who lived at an address in Hampstead. *Got you!*

***

From the drive, the house appeared to have been dropped out of a horror novel, with its high turrets and castellated frontage it had obviously been built in the Victorian Goth-ic period and Harker wouldn't have been too surprised to find a moat hiding behind the high hedged wall. He glanced tentatively at the intercom next to the railed gate toying with the idea of pressing it to ask if Miss Bathgate was in, but what excuse could he give? Even as a police officer he could not simply intrude on someone's privacy without good reason and furthermore there was no sign of her black BMW on the drive, *perhaps she wasn't in?* The constable regarded the large integral garage doors, *parked in there perhaps?* After pondering for a while Harker gave up and left to reconsider his strategy, completely unaware of being watched on a CCTV screen by a giant of a man wearing a butler's uniform.

As the sun began to set and his mistress rose from her slumber the faithful Renfield showed her the recorded footage, explaining. "I'm afraid I have no idea who he is ma'am."

"But I do, Renfield thank you for showing me this." *so Constable Harker, you have sought me out, what am I going to do with you?*

CHAPTER NINE - NINJA

"*All units, a woman's screams have been heard in the vicinity of the Old Brown Cow public house.*"

PC Greaves, who had just set out from Snow Hill, arrived just in time to see the black-clad figure dash back into the alley where a young woman was leaning against a wall, she had a look of terror on a face that was drenched with a dark fluid that could only be blood, but it wasn't hers, it belonged to the headless body lying at her feet.

"Bloody Nora!" exclaimed the WPC who had also responded.

"Stay with her Smithy, I'm after that bugger before he gets too far." With that Greaves set off down the cut-through. "PC4193 Greaves in pursuit of suspect down the alley next to the LSBM, requesting backup!" he was beginning to wish he hadn't rushed his pastrami bagel.

Smith was comforting the woman when a shadow loomed over them, startled, the policewoman looked up to see Sergeant Bathory.

"Sarge, Greavsie's gone after the suspect, that way!" the WPC pointed down the narrow passage.

The sergeant briefly examined the decapitated corpse

then stood and sniffed the air before disappearing into the dark alley after him without a word, leaving Smith with her charge.

Greaves emerged on Charterhouse Street and stopped to catch his breath. The mysterious fugitive had disappeared from sight and he thought he had lost them when movement caught his eye, a silhouette, framed in the city's night-time glow, was visible climbing onto the roof of the old meat market. After running across the road he stopped and looked in askance at the scaffold the fugitive had used to reach the roof of the building.

"Well, somebody has to go up after them." said a voice making him jump and he actually felt relieved to see the "Vampire" standing there.

"Sarge I err," he puffed.

Sirens could be heard and flashing lights were coming down the road, Bathory looked scornfully at his paunch. "Don't worry, I'll do it!" and after removing her non-issue high heels she swarmed up the scaffolding in stockinged feet.

Greaves was watching her climb over the edge and trying not to look too obviously at her long legs when a voice made him start for the second time.

"Who's up there?" asked Harker.

"Batty, she went up that scaffold like a bloody monkey!" he replied.

"You let her go on her own?"

"Jim I can't fucking climb that!" complained the corpulent policeman.

"Then you'd better give me a leg up, Greavsie."

Bathory was cautiously making her way across the shadowy world of the rooftops which was a veritable landscape of balustrades, cornices and mock turrets, the Victorian architect behind its design obviously had a large budget. She could smell the blood of the excised nosferatu and mingled with it was the scent of the spiker, who to her surprise was female. She could be anywhere, behind one of the cupolas or even the tall angled windows that allowed natural light into the building through frosted glass.

The vampire stopped and listened hearing a rapid heartbeat not too far away then a dark figure moved furtively out of the shadows towards the far end of the roof. "Stop police!" yelled Bathory.

The figure did stop and held something to her eye before producing what looked like a torch. Instantly guessing what it was, the vampire dived behind one of the glass tent-like structures but her hand, caught in the beam blistered as though burned, the fugitive was armed with a black lamp. *The bitch knew I was a vampyr!*

Elisabeth was gingerly examining her charred fingers where the skin was already beginning to regenerate, growing in from the undamaged areas when she heard someone approaching cautiously. *Was the spiker brave enough to come back in an attempt to excise her?*

"Sarge, your hand!" it was Harker. "Are you alright?"

"Fine Constable, the bastard had some kind of acid spray." she lied.

"I don't see anyone here now."

"We can't take that for granted, we'll split up and search but, Harker, be very careful."

"Backup is coming, shouldn't we wait for them?"

"The suspect will be long gone by the time they arrive, we must do it now," the pair searched the rooftop of the main building before crossing to the adjoining poultry market, but their quarry had vanished.

"Every where's linked up by little bridges," called Harker from the furthest edge of the roof. "The suspect could have gone anywhere, looks like we've lost them."

Upon returning to the main building it occurred to Bathory that the spiker had been empty-handed *and* she still detect a strong odour of vampire blood in the air, *the head, she's hidden it somewhere, somewhere the sun can do its work come morning.* The flesh and minor bones of a vampire burned easily under UV light, but the larger ones, including the skull, being of stronger construction, took longer to reduce to ash. Sniffing at the air again, Bathory followed the scent to one of the corner turrets close to where the spiker had emerged and spotted a dark stain on the stonework there.

"Constable Harker!" she called. "I need you!" Bathory climbed over and around a stone gryphon to stand shakily on a ledge and there it was jammed between one of the turret's windows and the elaborate wrought ironwork in front of it, eyes wide open and a grimace upon its fanged face, *the bitch must have stashed it here before I found her!* Holding the rail she lifted it out by the hair then balancing precariously, used the flat of her front door key to force the extended canines up into their sockets, *better the humans did not see that before Dee could claim the body*. She removed her uniform jacket and using it to wrap the decapitated head ,tossed it to Harker before scaling back over the gryphon and treating the surprised officer to an unexpected view as her skirt snagged on one of the mythical beast's wings.

"Come on Constable, let's see if your colleagues have had any luck apprehending our suspect, though I somehow doubt it!" she remarked, unashamedly smoothing down her clothing. *The Watchers church was less than a mile away, coincidence?*

"Sarge you've disturbed a crime scene!" complained the constable.

"Do you think I'm bothered?" she replied almost casually while examining the torn hose on her legs. "I'm going to claim for these, they're laddered to hell."

Back at ground level, Greaves took Harker to one side as Bathory reclaimed her heels. "Jim, Batty wears stockings and suspenders, I saw them when she climbed the scaffold."

"I know that already Greavsie and I've got news for you, she isn't wearing knickers either."

***

John Dee looked up from the folder. "So the attempted victim is a Maria Kieslowski who works as a barmaid at the Old Brown Cow?"

"Yes," replied Bathory sitting before his great oak desk. "A man, Peter Strickland had been chatting her up all night to no avail, after finishing her shift she set off for the tube when this Strickland put his hand over her mouth and dragged her into the nearby alleyway, when he ripped her blouse open she believed she was going to be raped, but of course it was to give him easy access to her neck. It was at this point Miss Kieslowski says the figure in black appeared, first stabbing Strickland in the chest with a pointed implement then beheading him with a single blow. I would say it's the work of an experienced spiker, most likely this fabled Van Helsing character."

"And you say this spiker is a woman?" asked Dee.

"Yes John, I could tell from the scent."

"Well, our tame human pathologist has examined the body, Strickland was stabbed once in the heart by a weapon of an unusual star-shaped cross-section before being decapitated by a very sharp blade, his remains will of course, be disposed of correctly and the police will be instructed on what to say. By the way, how is your hand?"

"It's healing well thank you." Bathory paused. "John, she knew I was undead, how?"

Dee became pensive. "Did the spiker have some kind of optical device?"

"Well, she did hold something to her eye before using the black light, why?"

The head of the Executive opened a drawer in his desk to produce a rose-coloured lens about fifty millimetres in diameter set in a gold mount and attached to a chain. "This is an Oculus Veritatis, one of only four in the world!" he announced.

"*The Eye of Truth*, I didn't believe they existed!"

Bathory was astonished, it was said that if you viewed a vampire through one their true nature would be revealed.

"Take a look." Dee tossed her the lens and Bathory caught it putting it to her eye, through the ruby glass the Doctor's stout, avuncular appearance became slightly translucent revealing a malign almost bat-like mien, his pointed fangs clearly visible.

"Is this what we are really like?" asked Bathory somewhat perturbed and holding out her hand which through the lens appeared thin and bony with fingernails like black claws. "I can see my talons!"

"Elisabeth, the crystal shows what is inside us. To be honest I wish we'd never had the damned things made."

"You had this made?"

He nodded. "My assistant Edward Kelley and I, with our families, toured Bohemia in search of occult knowledge and after studying reports and stories about the Nosferatu, determined to make a device which would enable people to see the demon lurking inside. We acquired a small flask of vampyr blood and recruited a certain glassmaker of renown in Warsaw, who, by mixing it into the glass while still molten, succeeded in creating a rose-coloured lens with remarkable properties. Sadly we also succeeded in attracting the attention of a certain Wallachian nobleman called Tepesh, who I believe you knew, he forced his company upon us and thought it great sport to turn the pair of us before stealing an oculus for himself. When he departed I fled to England with my unsuspecting family in tow, journeying only at night, of course. Upon my arrival home, I found my house ransacked and ruined but worse still, in the years I had been away my fair country had become intolerant of arcane study and practice. I quickly re-established my relations with good queen Gloriana and arranged to "die" sometime later. Edward however, risked everything by staying in Poland and did manage to sell one of the remaining oculi to King Stefan, who in turn presented it to the Pope to gain favour. The last oculus he kept for his own purposes but after being hunted down and excised by agents of the treacherous king it was lost." He took the lens wrapping it in its velvet cloth before adding. "Poor Edward was such a beautiful boy, but so headstrong and so foolhardy."

"In all the years I have known you John, why you have never mentioned this before?" asked Bathory, somewhat amazed.

"Shame, I suppose and think about it Elisabeth, if its existence was known the spikers might try to take it or even one of our own brethren." he looked crestfallen.

Bathory smiled and took his hand. "John, I'll tell no-one of this, I promise, oh and by the way Tepesh was my sire too, I found him a charming man and a passionate lover."

"Indeed he was" remarked Dee wistfully.

***

Christiana sat in her hotel room reflecting on last night's hunt, judging by the ease with which she had found the vampire the city must be teeming with the creatures. The undead policewoman had been somewhat of a surprise and because of her she'd had to dispose of the head in a hurry, *it had all been rather messy and she still hadn't heard a word about this vampire called Georgie, she would have to press her contacts further.*

CHAPTER TEN – DAYTIME

"Uncle Alan and Auntie Rose are coming down from Glasgow for a few days and they want to see me, so mum has asked me home for the weekend," announced Liz quickly.

Bathory had unexpectedly dropped in to avoid the imminent dawn, forgetting it was the nurse's day shift. "How long will you be away?"

"Friday to Sunday, you don't mind do you, I suppose you could come but it might be difficult, they don't know I'm gay and with you being a vampire?"

"You go and see your relatives, my love, I'm getting fed up seeing with your ugly face anyway" teased Elisabeth, peering in Liz' refrigerator.

"You skinny pasty-faced bitch, I might find someone better in Wakefield and not come back!" retorted Liz in kind.

"How would a chubby little Goth like you find another vampyr as beautiful as me?" she popped a piece of raw steak into her mouth.

"Chubby?"

Bathory enfolded her partner in her arms. "Plenty to hold on to!" she moved her hands down and they began to smooch.

"Ugh your breath smells of raw meat!"

"I could put my mouth somewhere else." Elisabeth slid her hand into Liz's waistband, feeling for the zip with the other.

"Oh no, Beth, I really don't have time, I need to get to work!" she reluctantly freed herself from the embrace.

"We'll perhaps have time tonight before I go out on patrol?" she smiled toothily.

"You're going out again, are things that bad?" her lover had shared a little of the current situation with her.

"Things have gotten worse, there's a spiker loose somewhere in the city." *I mustn't tell her anything else, she'll only worry.*

"Spikers kill vampires don't they?" asked Liz with concern.

Elisabeth nodded.

"Oh please take care I couldn't stand it if anything happened to you."

"I'll be fine, the sun's up soon so I'll have to stay here anyway, I'll run us a nice bath when you get back this afternoon and then I'll eat you," stated the vampire with a grin.

"Promise?" asked Liz with a smile.

"Promise!" replied Bathory.

"It's such a bugger you not being able to go out in daylight, I'd hate it!"

"You don't fancy being a vampyr then?"

"No! I like being normal!" she thought about what she had just said. "Sorry, Beth I didn't mean that nastily."

"Don't worry, I've had centuries to get used to things like that." *she was right though, it was a bugger sometimes!*

Liz gave her a long lingering kiss despite the meat breath. "There's blood in the fridge if you're peckish, see you later."

Before retiring for a day's sleep, Elisabeth switched on the television to catch the media's take on last night's events, as she watched the official lies being repeated by the newsreader her mind wandered to the nurse. Their relationship had been purely sexual to begin with, but she was beginning to care and knew Liz felt far more in return, she had fallen in love with humans before only to watch them age and die while she remained unchanged and every time it had broken her heart and every time she had promised herself not to let it happen again.

***

Harker lay in his bed unable to get Bathory out of his mind, she had the most incredible legs and the rest of her lower half was pretty good as he could attest to. He found himself aroused at the memory of the sergeant's unexpected exposure, desperately he tried to put it to the back of his mind and go to sleep but it was to no avail, the memory of her nether regions would not let him rest so finally giving in to desire he took himself in hand to seek relief. Later as he drifted off to sleep a thought crossed his mind, *how old is Sergeant Bathory?*

Chapter Eleven - Cocktails

"Where are we going?" asked Liz.

"One of my favourite watering-holes, I haven't been there for ages." The past couple of nights had been quiet so Bathory had decided to take her partner for an evening out.

"What's it called?"

"Liddell's," replied Bathory.

"That's a supermarket, Toothy!" laughed Liz.

"Different spelling, Chunky!" retorted Elisabeth pinching the nurse's well-upholstered derriere.

As soon as they entered the swish establishment Liz felt awkward, her leather mini-dress and jet black hair did not sit well with all the designer fashion on display. Bathory, of course, looked fabulous in a dark red cocktail dress but then, to Liz, she couldn't look anything else. "I feel a little out of place Beth, all these fashionistas, it makes me feel uncomfortable."

"Fuck 'em," replied Bathory staring down a city type ogling her long legs as she sat on a high bar stool.

"What would like you to drink ladies?" asked the bartender.

"Karl these are my customers, you go and serve that miserable pair over there." a short man with a receding hairline had appeared and gesturing towards the afore-mentioned couple whispered. "He's not bad-looking but that woman in the business suit, ugh nothing matches, shoes, handbag… face."

"Hello Skinner, long time, no see," said Bathory smiling warmly.

"Ah the lovely Bess, it's been months since I last saw you!" he kissed her hand flamboyantly and then turning to Liz extended her the same courtesy saying. "And you've brought the missus too?"

"Eh?" said Liz trying not to stare at his pointed canines.

"Oh don't try to deny it, love, you're so her type, our Bess likes her men thin and her women not so!" he looked meaningfully at Bathory. "No offence meant dear, but it's the truth ain't it?"

"Mmm, Liz, meet Albert Skinner, proprietor of this sad excuse for a gin palace."

He grinned toothily. "Known as the "Camp Vamp" to those what know me, her ladyship must think very highly of you Liz, she don't bring just any old piece of fluff to Liddell's. Now, Bess, you'll be wanting the usual I take it?" Bathory nodded. "And lovely Liz, what would you like? Name it and if we ain't got it I'll send the gorgeous Karl out for it."

"I've always wanted to try a Cosmopolitan."

"Ooh, how Sex and the City are you?" Skinner busied himself with the shaker and produced a pink concoction with a twist of orange peel. "It's on the house since it's your first time, if you don't like it I'll mix you an Espresso Martini, right on vogue with the coffee culture and a favourite of mine" he produced a gory red drink for Bathory. "A Bloody Hell for you, madam."

"Is that like a Bloody Mary?" asked Liz.

"Sort of, only really, really bloody," replied Elisabeth licking a red drip from her lips.

"Eh… Oh I wish I hadn't asked," stated Liz as the penny dropped.

"Some amuse-bouche for the ladies?" the bar owner reappeared with a couple of plates and addressing Liz said. "Now pay attention human, most of this is safe for you to eat, but I would advise against the Red Hot Jellies."

"Ugh, I'll pass thank you, Mr Skinner, how do you know Beth?" she asked as the woman in question picked up a cube of whatever it was.

"You don't need to know, wow, how much chilli is in this?" Bathory spluttered.

"Just a smidgeon," he smiled as Bathory gulped down the water he offered. "In Georgian times Bawdy Bess here kept one of the best brothels in old London town, staffed entirely by very able vampyr girls and it is reckoned that John Cleland based a character in Fanny Hill on her."

"Not true I never met the man!" Elisabeth protested. "I did know Defoe though."

"He wrote Moll Flanders!" exclaimed Liz. "I've seen that one on the telly."

"Read Fanny Hill and look out for Mrs Cole, she's only half of what your Bess was mind," said Skinner with a grin.

"You ran a seedy gin shop not too far from here as I seem to recall," said Bathory.

"I did indeed, they were fun times for us undead." agreed Skinner.

"Wow you've known each other that long?" asked Liz.

"Hundreds of years, Bess looks good in a powdered wig and corset, mind you, I could always turn a better ankle than her."

"Weren't those things supposed to be full of lice?"

"Not a problem for the undead my darling, lice, in common with all nature's creatures tend to give us a wide berth," replied Bathory.

"Yeah, something to do with that symbiotic whatsit in our blood," stated Skinner. "Makes us taste unpleasant to them, it's only you humans who are too daft to notice."

While Skinner discussed the finer points of the vampiric condition with Liz, Bathory cast an eye out of the window to see two police officers walking by, one was very familiar.

"There goes Lily Law!" remarked Skinner on seeing them.

"They're from Bishopsgate, the man's Harker and I think the WPC is Jackson," said Elisabeth, *Harker is quite handsome.* "Any of the other brethren been in here tonight?" asked Bathory changing the subject.

"No you're the only one so far, you're not out on the prowl yourself then?"

"No I'm having a night off, since that Strickland fellow lost his head there have been no more humans killed, at least not by vampyrs."

"Ooh you've just reminded me that there's that spiker still at large, I don't much fancy my neck being severed" remarked the bar owner.

Who does? Thought Liz …

***

"Oh my god, you're on form tonight," Liz was in postorgasmic bliss, her lover had just played a symphony on her with her tongue.

"Glad to be of service," laughed Elisabeth, they were both somewhat drunk.

"Do you need any blood my love?" asked the younger woman.

"No, I had enough at Albert's place."

"That red jelly stuff was blood, wasn't it?" asked Liz

"Yes but it was beef not human, Skinner was winding you up."

"It's still disgusting, you know Beth I find your unlife a little disturbing at times."

"Can't be helped, that's who I am," she replied.

"You're not cross with me for earlier on, are you?" asked Liz

"If I was cross with you would I have just done that?" she replied, after leaving Liddell's, they had walked down to the riverfront to stand for a while arms around one another while looking at the Thames with the lights illuminating Tower Bridge and HMS Belfast moored nearby.

"Look at us." Liz had laughed. "A short fat Goth with a tall blonde vampire, what must we look like?"

"You're not fat, you're just not so thin like Albert said, well perhaps a bit chubby" joked Bathory.

"Skinny bitch, you're going to wake up with a stake through your heart one day!" was her riposte.

Bathory had hugged her close then said awkwardly. "Liz we've been together for a while and I care for you a lot, would you let me?"

"Oh god, you're going to ask me to marry you aren't you?"

"No not that, turn you?"

"What does that mean, turn me?" asked the nurse, slightly disappointed and now a little concerned.

"Turn you into a vampyr, like me" Bathory had replied

"No!" Liz had said without hesitation.

"But..." Bathory had begun.

"No buts, the answer is no!" she had said firmly. They had walked to St Paul's tube station in silence but once back inside her flat they shared a passionate reconciliatory kiss which ended with Elisabeth lifting Liz in her arms and carrying her to the bedroom.

"Why don't you want to be a vampyr?" asked Elisabeth nuzzling her neck.

"What apart from not being able to go out in daylight

and having to drink blood?"

"You would never age, never die and we could be together forever."

"I'm a nurse, we don't hurt people."

"You don't have to hurt them just take a bit of the red stuff occasionally."

"Er, kind of know that, Toothy. How does it work then, turning someone?"

"You drink my blood then the symbiont takes hold and you turn into a vampyr."

"Just like that?" asked Liz.

"Hematophagy is instant, as are the enhanced senses but it takes a couple of days for your physiology to alter, your teeth change very quickly, other things come later," she explained.

"So, would I have to bite you?"

"It has to be fresh from the donor or it will just make you really ill, I can open a wound myself if you don't want to?" explained Bathory.

"Would I have to bite your throat?" *I can't believe I'm even asking this.*

"Throat, wrist, inner thigh perhaps?" she raised her eyebrow at the last suggestion. "Call it the ultimate love bite."

"Would it hurt, Beth?"

"It would sting a bit but I'd heal quickly, though it does take it out of you if you do it too often."

"My answer's still no, the mere thought of something living inside me and making me drink blood scares me."

"Vampyrism doesn't live in you darling, it becomes you and you become it, that's why it's called symbiosis."

"You're talking to a trained professional, I know what symbiosis is and it's not quite that!"

"You would still be you, just a stronger better version. I would never force it on you, I promise."

"Maybe when I'm older before my arse sags too much." she felt her way down the vampire's lissom body, probing with delicate fingers.

Bathory obligingly moved her thighs apart. "Well, the offer's still open whenever you want to, oh!"

Liz had found what she was seeking and began to circle it with a moistened finger. "We'll see." their lips met briefly before Bathory lay back to enjoy her lover's attention while trying hard not to think of a certain young policeman.

CHAPTER TWELVE – WARNING

"Good Morning John, sorry to raise you from your coffin," said the voice on the phone, it was redolent of public school and had a sinister quality.

"Er, it's no problem Secretary, you do know we don't really sleep in coffins, don't you?" answered Dee, he didn't know the man's name he was the latest in a long line of Secretaries appointed over the centuries. Some had been quite personable, this one wasn't.

"Ha-ha just my little joke!" replied the voice mirthlessly.

"To what do I owe this pleasure, Secretary?"

"Doctor Dee, I have had a complaint from the Chief Constable that an office in Whitehall has been interfering in their investigations, claiming bodies and telling her what to say to the press. I assume you have a good reason for this?"

"Yes, one of our own was involved and we are taking measures to prevent it from happening again."

"Good, I have, of course, examined the facts for myself and if you say you have the matter in hand I am happy to leave you to your own devices, I wouldn't want to upset the applecart as it were."

"Thank you Secretary, I hope we saw the end to it last night."

"Ah yes, the sword-wielding vigilante, a shame your Enforcer didn't catch him."

"Indeed, the spiker was well prepared against our kind."

"Spiker, yes that's what you call us when we terminate you isn't it, do you know where this spiker heralds from?" asked the civil servant.

"From the Low Countries, we believe."

"Now that is interesting, they have very few vampires over there and there are so many here."

"Yes but we follow the Edict and live alongside humanity in peace," Dee wondered where this was going.

"You hide amongst us while taking our blood, what an interesting definition of peace, still if you've got this situation under control I won't keep you from your sleep any longer" he hung up.

Dee sat looking at the telephone receiver in his hand, was that a threat or a warning? *One thing was for certain, sleep was out of the question now!"*

CHAPTER THIRTEEN - DINNER

To Harker's disgruntlement, Sergeant Bathory had not been to the station for a while and there hadn't been another death since the incident at the Cow. *Perhaps the masked swordsman with the flair for the dramatic had finished the job for them?*

A cough drew his attention and there she was, looking in the sliding window.

"On desk duty tonight James?" she asked with her perfect mouth, pink tongue visible behind white, slightly too pointed teeth.

For a moment he just stared speechlessly, *stop it you, idiot!* "Afraid so Sarge, things have been rather quiet since the Ninja killed that rapist."

"The Ninja?" she asked, her brown eyes drawing him in.

"That's what the newspapers are calling him, treating him like he's some kind of hero."

"I don't want to piss on your cornflakes, James, but this *Ninja* is a killer and is still at large *and* I fear it's not going to be too long before we hear from them again!" she asserted.

"You're right of course Sarge, I'll let you in."

"No need to James, I just came in to see you, you're not busy tomorrow night by any chance?" she raised her eyebrows slightly.

"No I've got two days off," he replied, craning his neck in an attempt to spot if the woman had a reflection in the glass of the noticeboard.

"Funnily enough so have I." stated Bathory with a wink. "I'll pick you up outside your flat at eight-thirty."

As she walked towards the door he called. "But you don't know where I live?"

"Oh yes I do" she replied.

***

Harker came out of his flat to find Bathory leaning against her shiny black car. She was wearing a dark green dress, her bare legs ended in high heels and her long, surprisingly wavy platinum blonde hair cascaded loosely about her shoulders. He felt a slight concern about why this vision of beauty should be interested in him. *It almost seemed too good to be true?*

"Wow, Sarge, you look amazing!" exclaimed Harker.

With her partner away for the weekend, Bathory had decided it was time to spread her wings, Liz had refused to be turned and she so didn't want to fall in love with a mortal again, *so perhaps a fling would cure her of her feelings.* Not only that this rather good-looking officer had been taking a lot of interest in her and it was time she found out why.

"Thank you, James, you don't look so bad yourself and my name is Elisabeth remember?"

"Okay, Elisabeth where are we going?"

"Get in and you'll see."

Bathory drove through the city streets at a breakneck pace with the journey finally ending in an underground car park, when they emerged Harker looked about in uncertainty. "Where are we, somewhere near Baker Street?"

"Salisbury Mews not far off, I thought I'd take you somewhere rather different."

They entered a rundown pub called The Cursed Blacksmith to be scrutinised by the stony-faced barman and after satisfying his curiosity he reached under the counter. A hidden door in the wall clicked open and the couple stepped through to a large room where they were confronted by two huge men in fancy uniform. Bathory glared at the bouncers and one grunted, opening a further door leading into what looked like the set of a gothic horror movie. The walls appeared to be made of rough stone adorned with chains and manacles, burning torches were set in sockets at regular intervals. After Bathory spoke with a painfully thin man they were escorted by a buxom kirtle-wearing waitress through a bustling room, furnished with wooden tables occupied by diners who looked as if they'd escaped from a 1980's music video and into a quiet corridor of curtained booths.

After showing the couple into an unoccupied cubicle she handed them a large menu. "What is this place?" asked Harker in hushed tones when they were alone.

"It's a rather exclusive restaurant frequented by expats, the bouncers didn't recognise you but they know better than to argue with me."

"What's this place supposed to be, a castle in Transylvania?" he laughed nervously.

"Hollywood's interpretation of one I think. I knew the area well and don't remember anything remotely like this," she replied.

Harker was puzzled at her use of past tense. "Where are you from then Sarge, somewhere in Eastern Europe?"

"Hungary, but I expect it's changed a lot since I last was there."

"How long ago was that?" he asked.

"Oh quite a while," she replied evasively.

The waitress reappeared brandishing two large ornate

flagons, one contained water and the other what appeared to be red wine, Harker reached for the *wine*.

"No not that!" snapped Bathory before barking something at the waitress in what was probably Hungarian. "Sorry for my little outburst James, you would not enjoy that, it is very much an acquired taste. I've ordered a bottle of Merlot for you, will that be alright or is there anything else you would like, they do a good range of East European beers?"

"Merlot will be fine thank you Elisabeth" he watched as she poured herself a glass of the opaque red liquid, *she can't really be a vampire, can she?*

The menu was ludicrously expensive but Elisabeth insisted it was on her, James watched her tearing into the lobster starter with her sharp teeth, licking the juice off her red lips with her pink tongue while imagining what else she could do with it. *Bloody hell, her eating is turning me on!*

"Do you know you're the first person who's not of our kind I've brought here, others do it all the time but I never have," she confessed as the plates were cleared away.

"By our kind you do mean expats?" *or vampires?*

"Yes, not even my girlfriend has been here," Elisabeth felt a pang of guilt at the mention, *it would pass*. She took a large swig from her glass.

Harker, who had been nursing an erection, felt his hopes falling. "Girlfriend, Sarge I didn't know you were..?"

"A lesbian?" she finished his sentence for him. "My partner is the gay one, I just don't have boundaries."

"Oh, so you are interested in men too?"

"Yes of course I am, did you like what you saw the other night James?" she asked coquettishly.

"Er, I didn't mean to look, Sarge, I couldn't help it but yes I liked it, er..." he spluttered remembering the sight of her womanhood with its pale curls.

"I'm not ashamed of my body James it's served me well for many years," she assured him.

"How many years?" he asked admiring the swell of

her bosom, erect nipples visible under the thin material of her dress.

"I'm a lot older than you perhaps think, call me a cougar if you like, you people nowadays have such interesting descriptions," she laughed lightly. "Were there ever sabre-toothed cougars, you know, like tigers?"

"I don't know?" he replied. Bathory was watching him intently, reminding Harker of a lioness studying its prey.

"James, what were you doing outside my house the other day?" she inquired in a purr that had just a touch of razor-sharp steel to it.

He flushed red. "Sarge, I don't want to sound like a weirdo but I'm genuinely fascinated by you, you're like no-one I've ever met before and then there's that name and the other night when you…" *he'd blown it surely?*

She smiled. "It is somewhat odd behaviour on your part perhaps, James, if you fancied me why did you not say so before. I have brought you here for a reason do I have to spell out why?"

The waitress arrived with the main course saving him from answering. He had chosen goulash, the house speciality, a fiery beef stew made with hot paprika and tomatoes, served with noodles and sour cream on the top. Hers was steak tartare, a melange made with a ground fillet, capers, shallots and various herbs, all served uncooked on a large slice of rye bread with a raw egg cracked over it.

"Was that good?" Harker asked curiously after she had devoured it, washing it down with more of the dark red *wine*.

"Mmm, I love red meat," she replied bathing him with a look from her brown eyes, he jumped as something touched his crotch. Bathory, now quite intoxicated had kicked off her shoes and was running a toe around his tumescence. "Talking of which, how about we skip dessert and concentrate on this evening's main event?"

"Sarge er, Elisabeth?" he ought not to ask but it was

burning inside him. "Are you a vampire?"

She put down her glass and smiled exposing all of her very sharp looking teeth. "That's not a sensible question to ask someone who's about to put their mouth around your cock!" ducking beneath the table she unzipped his flies to release his not inconsiderable erection then undid his trousers and began pulling at them.

"Oh god!" he exclaimed as she ran her tongue along the length of his shaft, he felt her nibbling lightly at it.

She stopped briefly and her voice came from under the table. "The dorsal artery is just along the top of the penis and if I were a vampire all I would have to do is sink my fangs in just here." After briefly touching her tongue on it and to his great relief, she enveloped his glans with her lips to fellate him briefly before emerging sinuously from under the table, pushing it back and at the same time slipping her dress from her shoulders, shrugging it off like a beautiful snake shedding its skin. Bathory's body was pale perfection like a marble statue with neatly curled pubic hair, she mounted his penis, riding him hard to reach a climax as he ejaculated into her, then pulling open Harker's white shirt she pressed her naked bosom against his chest. "More!" she purred into his ear while drawing her fingernails down his leg to leave red marks, she cupped his balls in her hand. "More!"

"Elisabeth, a moment please." he gasped.

"Here is the answer to your question James, I am a vampyr, people used to call me the Blood Countess and you will do as I ask!" extending her fangs she bit him on the neck, his ardour returned with a vengeance and he did exactly as he was asked, several times in as many different ways as the confines of the small booth would allow.

***

Harker woke alone in his own bed with an aching groin. It was eleven o'clock in the morning, *had he dreamt all that?*

The answer to his question came as Elisabeth walked into the bedroom clad in only the shirt he wore last night, small spots of red were visible on the collar. "I've made you breakfast," she announced passing him a tray with coffee and warmed croissants.

He looked in surprise at the pastries.

"I got the taxi-driver to stop at an all-night bakery on the way back from The Cursed Blacksmith, I didn't expect a single man wouldn't have much more than cereal in his cupboards, oh and by the way if you expect me to stay over in future there is to be no more garlic sausage in the fridge, I nearly puked when I opened it."

"Sarge, I'm a bit confused, did you bite me last night?"

She continued unabashed. "And your curtains are a bit thin for my liking they let in far too much daylight."

He looked at the shirt with its blood-stained collar and frowned. "Elisabeth, did you bite me last night?" he asked again.

"I'm a vampyr that's what we do" she replied lightly.

Oh god, it wasn't a dream! "Will I become like you?"

She sat on the bed next to him and finding her phone texted Renfield to pick up her car. "No idiot, you can't get Vampyrism just from me biting you and anyway, it's not the first time I've tasted your blood."

"What!"

Bathory put her hand on his cheek and gazed deeply into his eyes to command. "Remember the night of our first meeting!"

The events of the body in the alley came rushing back to him. "You made me forget you were there, why?"

"Would you rather I'd killed you when I accidentally revealed my true nature?"

"But, but you're like a normal person?" he spluttered.

"James, vampyrs are portrayed either as cold-hearted monsters or love-sick teenagers but we are just like you, there are good and bad within the brethren just as with humans."

Yeah, but we don't drink other people's blood! He asked aloud. "So are you really a policewoman?"

"Sort of, I enforce the Edict."

"Edict, brethren, this all sounds very organised how many vampires are there?"

"Not that many James we are a hidden people, we have colonies in most major cities throughout the world."

"Just the cities?" asked Harker.

"Mainly, we prefer to be anonymous and it is so much easier to unlive somewhere where the population always fluctuates, everyone is a stranger in a city, there are plenty of places to hide from the daylight and as long as we don't kill our prey no-one is the wiser."

Harker didn't much like the idea of being thought of as prey. "And your job as an enforcer is to make sure no-one dies?"

"One hundred and forty years ago the brethren of this country decreed that no vampyr should take more blood than is needed for sustenance. The penalties for transgression are severe, you can be exiled for taking too much and for deliberately bleeding a human to death the penalty can be excision, the popular human term is slaying I believe?"

"This is something of a shock Elisabeth, I sort of wondered if you were a *vampire* but this is a bit hard to take in."

She perched on the bed arms around her knees, looking just like a normal woman. "We're not that different? I was human once and still have human desires and feelings, I like to drink, not just blood and watch TV, go to the cinema, go to nightclubs, as long as they don't have UV lights, of course."

"That Cursed Blacksmith place, it's just for vampires, isn't it?"

"Yes, there are several venues exclusively for creatures of the night around London, we are allowed to bring humans as pets. The doormen thought you were my pet," she informed him.

"Pet?"

"Plaything and occasional food-source, James I'm not like them I don't do that to humans."

"Shit, that's exactly what you did to me though!" *was this partner of hers a pet?*

Bathory nuzzled up to him. "Sorry, I did get carried away, too many Blood Vodkas."

That must have been the red stuff in the flask. "Then you are the real Elisabeth Bathory?"

She nodded.

"That would make you about four hundred and fifty years old!" he exclaimed.

"Closer to four hundred and sixty but I don't keep count."

"Elisabeth, those gory stories about you, is there any truth in them?" *careful, she bit you after you asked if she was a vampire.*

"Most are exaggerated, a lot was made up by my accusers but I was an unpleasant person and after turning I killed a great many people for blood."

"And they bricked you up in your rooms?"

Bathory laughed bitterly. "They couldn't excise me because of my high born position so I was imprisoned in *my* own chambers, in *my* own castle, the fools didn't realise I had a secret exit in case someone wanted to assassinate me."

"And you escaped?"

"I should have done there and then but I was furious at being betrayed and went out nightly to wreak my revenge on the local populace, including the priest who had brought the original accusation. My guards might have been slow on the uptake but they did work it out after a few days and set watch on the slot they passed food through and one night they were waiting outside with the bastard who prosecuted me, after breaking every bone in my body they shut me in a simple coffin and buried it in the middle of the forest. I lay there in complete darkness for four agonising years almost going mad and unable to heal for lack of fresh blood. My faithful servant Katrina eventually escaped from prison and upon discovering my burial place had me disinterred, I see my torment as just punishment for what I had inflicted on others."

"And then you escaped?"

"Not immediately, the hired sexton removed the lid and as he bent over my open coffin Katrina took him by surprise and pulled his head back to slit open his throat allowing the blood to wash over me. It was not nearly enough so she opened her wrist and held it to my mouth allowing me to bleed her dry, I managed to pull the lid back over the casket before the sun rose and lay there healing, trapped only by the sunlight. Come dark, I emerged from my grave to find poor Katrina had brought fresh clothes to replace my rotting rags and a pouch of gold coins from a hidden cache. I gave her a decent burial in my old coffin and after covering it once again staggered from the forest to burst into the first hovel I found. The occupants were a poor mother and her children, the husband away fighting the Turks. She must have guessed what I was but shared their meagre meal with me regardless but it didn't staunch the hunger inside me, I wanted blood and she had two children. I remember thinking that she wouldn't miss the youngest and demanded it from her but the woman threw herself at my feet begging I take her instead, for the second time in as many days a human was willingly offering me their life! I looked at the children cowering in fear and felt pity for the first time in many years, after throwing down a gold coin in front of the cowering woman I stumbled out into the night leaving the family unscathed. After slaking my thirst on a tethered cow further down the road I spent the day hidden under straw in a nearby barn. The farmer finding his prize animal bleeding from a neck wound raised the alarm and when I woke I had to flee for my unlife. My original intention had been to head westwards, but first there was a task to complete and hunting down my prosecutor I turned him so that he might be pursued as I was. The Great Purge of the East was by now underway led by the hateful spikers under the sponsorship of the church, those of us that fled survived, those who stayed were excised and the East-European vampyrs were hunted almost to extinction. I spent the next hundred years running and hiding to finally arrive in England at the start of the eighteenth century when society was so amoral and debauched," she smiled at the memory.

Harker was fascinated. "So you reached England and became a vampire cop?"

Bathory shook her head. "No, the Victorians came along with their pious hypocrisy followed by the re-emergence of the spikers, only now well well-educated and highly trained. One particularly diligent spiker from the Low Countries even managed to excise Tepesh after he had re-established his presence in Transylvania. A secret war raged all through the nineteenth century until your Scotland Yard approached us to offer a truce if we excised the Whitechapel Murderer, one of our own who had gone beyond blood-crazy. In the peace that followed, Dr John Dee proposed the Edict and we disappeared into legend with only the very highest level of your Civil Service knowing of our existence."

"So the government know all about you?"

"I didn't say anything about the government, did I?" she smiled grimly. "Now someone is encouraging the killing of humans again, someone who I believe wants things back to how they were hundreds of years ago."

"The body in the alleyway!" exclaimed Harker in realisation, she nodded. "And this Ninja is a spiker?" she nodded again. "Elisabeth, how did you become a vampire?"

"Vlad Tepesh came to me seeking sanctuary, having

been driven out of Wallachia and hearing of my blood-thirsty nature he threw himself on my mercy. The man was so charismatic that I fell for him becoming first his lover and then at my request made me a vampyr too."

"Vlad Tepesh!" interjected Harker. "You mean Dracula?"

"Yes, Dracula the son of the Devil, he was a heroic leader who fought the invading Turks but all people want to remember is the blood and the stakes, things were so very different back then, life was very brutal and equally short." She moved her lips closer to his. "Would you like to be a vampyr James?"

"No not really," he answered nervously, her eyes were like dark pools and he was struggling not to fall into them.

"Okay!" she kissed him quickly, then sitting up and smiling grabbed one of his hands to put it under the shirt she was wearing.

He cupped a breast feeling the nipple stand up at his touch. "Wait, if I'm not a pet and you're not going to turn me into a vampire then what am I and please don't say lunch?" he could see her teeth and was both scared and excited at what she might do next.

"Let's call you an interesting distraction" Bathory sat astride him and peeled the bloodstained shirt over her head...

Chapter Fourteen - Gervase

Dee sat on a bench under the twinkling stars at the edge of the heath and with Highgate Cemetery to his back, had a clear view of the city's bright lights. *Elisabeth lives somewhere near here* thought Dee, he pondered about how pleasant it would be to be able to visit during the daytime, the heath was a jewel in the heart of the conurbation, there were other green areas dotted around London but this side of the Thames there was no single one as large as Hampstead Heath. Some people wouldn't be seen dead here after dark because of the reputation it had garnered over the years but Dee wasn't concerned, he occasionally frequented the area to find both diversion and refreshment among the nocturnal populace.

A man in dark clothes sat down on the opposite end of the bench and asked. "Why do you pick such dire places to meet?"

"Am I not a creature of the night, Father Gervase?" he replied.

Gervase was the founder of the Watchers, an offshoot

of the church that preached long and loud about the hidden danger of the *blood-soaked undead,* the Executive left usually them to their own devices as most people believed they were crazy and on a par with Flat-Earthers or other such conspiracy theorists, nevertheless they did have a small corps of devotees.

Occasionally, Dee would meet with their leader to assure that all was fine with the Edict and they weren't going to start slaughtering the innocent in their beds, Gervase was one of the few Watchers who had actually seen vampires in the *flesh* as it were and even claimed to have excised one in Spain.

"This sudden increase in death by savage exsanguination is helping our cause considerably Dr Dee and more people are coming to our sermons, the continued existence of your unholy kind upon God's earth may soon be drawing to a close!" there was a hint of smugness in his voice.

"Brave words Father, please come no closer I can smell the garlic on your breath from here, it is quite nauseating."

"A necessary precaution I feel, as is the black lamp I carry."

"And the man standing in the shadows with the crossbow is too, I suppose?"

The priest nodded. "You are a perceptive creature indeed, so what is it you want?"

"I have information that there is a spiker at large in the city, a woman?" explained Dee.

"I have heard something to that effect" Gervase certainly had, he was Christiana's contact in London and had arranged her accommodation as well as supplying information about vampire activity in the city.

"If you were to have seen this spiker, would you know what her reason was for being here?"

The priest smiled. "Well, I *have* heard a rumour."

CHAPTER FIFTEEN - MCGREGOR

"So are you and that old bitch a thing then?"

"Eh?" asked Harper in surprise.

"You went out with *Batty Bathory* the other night," said Jenny Jackson accusingly, it was her turn on the desk tonight.

The constable had been on his way out but stopped to lean in the hatch. "She took me to a weird theme restaurant, that's all."

"Did you shag her?"

"Hey, Jen I'm not answering that!"

"That means you did! Bloody hell, Jim, she must be nearly fifty, what do you see in her?"

Add about four hundred years. "She's an attractive woman Jen, what's it to you anyway?"

"Nothing!" she looked disconcerted.

"Redmond's right, you do fancy me don't you?"

"Shut up and get out on your beat Harker."

"Jen, I had no idea?" he hadn't *and* he liked the dark officer himself, quite a lot.

"Perhaps I should walk around with a sign on my

head?" she almost smiled then her face fell, Bathory was walking in the front door.

"Ah James, just about to go out the beat?" she took in the tableau formed by the conversing officers. "Not disturbing anything, am I?"

"No Sarge, Constable Harker's just setting off, aren't you Jim?" answered Jackson sourly.

"Good, then I will walk with you a while." asserted Bathory and the pair left the station with Jackson glaring at them.

"WPC Jackson is a pretty girl" remarked Bathory as they walked along Bishopsgate. "She doesn't like me though, does she?"

"You're a bit intimidating, that's all."

"That's very noble of you, James she dislikes me because she thinks I have you."

"Is this some kind of vampire intuition?" he asked.

"It's called being a woman you idiot, why don't you ask her out?"

"What, I thought we were..?"

"James, I only want you for sex, most young men would jump at the chance."

He grinned in response *it was almost too good to be true.*

Bathory took his hand to lead him down a narrow alley between two buildings then leaned up against a wall and hoisted her skirt. "Do I have to bite you again or are you going to do this on your own?" Harker didn't need to be asked twice and took Elisabeth against the wall while she wrapped her stockinged thighs around his waist.

They had adjusted their clothes and returned to the brightly lit street when a broad Scottish voice boomed. "Lizzie, I've been looking for you everywhere!"

She grinned broadly showing sharp teeth. "Rob, what are you doing still in London?"

He gave her an equally pointy smile. "John sent me to look for you, he said you were planning to start at Bishopsgate tonight." he noticed Harker. "Hullo, what's this?"

"PC Harker sir!" he replied, the man, obviously a vampire, wore an inspector's uniform.

"It's James he's a friend, *who knows and understands!*" Bathory informed the tall red-haired man.

"Oh, I see, well Constable I need to speak to Lizzie, er, Sergeant Bathory in private." Harker taking the hint went off on his beat with a spring in his step. McGregor watched him walk away. "He's only a wee young lad, can you trust him?"

"James can't tell anyone, he doesn't realise it but I've entranced him," she replied. "And I top him up regularly as it were."

"So Miss Sanctimonious has created a thrall of her own?"

"No, he is not my thrall, I just keep his interest up," she replied slightly embarrassed. "and he services me in return if you must know."

McGregor grinned widely. "I thought you favoured lassies nowadays?"

"Just keeping my options open, you know me?"

"Aye, I still hold a torch for you meself, Lizzie, I treasure the time we spent together."

"We had fifty years Rob, wasn't that long enough?"

He shrugged. "Anyways, the good doctor thinks you need some backup with things being the way they are, so I've brought a few of the clan down from over the border."

"Thanks, Rob, I've always been able to manage the city single-handed and I don't usually need help but something's building up, I can feel it."

"John thinks you should have a regular company of Enforcers as I have in Glasgow and Edinburgh."

"I don't often turn people and no-one has ever volunteered to join." she had deputised vampires in the past but they were only ever temporary postings.

"You could start with that young copper?" mused McGregor.

"No fucking way am I turning James into a vampyr."

perhaps a new assistant would be useful, she had Renfield, of course, but he was only good as muscle.

"You should, your own turnees are always loyal to you," suggested McGregor.

"I turned Thurzo remember, he fucking isn't?"

"Point taken, there's always the exception that proves the rule. By the way, you know Dee's human liaison is sabre-rattling, don't you?" McGregor asked.

"Yes and you and I both know that Thurzo's behind all this trouble?"

"But why create so few at a time why not build an army?"

"Come on Rob you know how turning takes it out of you, not only that he's looking to destabilise our relations with the living while swaying as many elders as possible to his side at the same time, too many deaths and they might get twitchy."

The vampire nodded. "You may well be right Lizzie, but proving it is going to be a bugger."

***

On the floor of a tiled room in Whitechapel, a young man opened his eyes sat up sharply and hissed showing canines that were already becoming pointed. A hooded figure entered carrying a tall cup of crimson liquid which was proffered to the man, who snatched it greedily drinking down its contents.

"Good you're nearly ready." said the voice of the cupbearer. "No more free meals for you I'm afraid, Leo, tomorrow night you hunt for yourself but don't worry you'll find plenty of unsuspecting prey out there."

CHAPTER SIXTEEN – VICTIMS

Adeline Murray's body was found under the cupola of the memorial fountain in Victoria Tower Gardens, Bathory responded as fast as she could and then had to argue with a Detective Inspector Scanlon who was outraged that *he* had been ordered to wait for a uniformed WPS to attend. Dee had once asked Bathory why she had picked such a lowly rank, she replied that it allowed her unbridled freedom of movement around the city while generating immediate trust in the public and she quite enjoyed wearing the uniform, or her variant of it.

This latest victim was a young woman who worked as a high-class escort and had been discovered with her throat ripped open in the usual manner of blood-rage. Elisabeth could detect the scent of the perpetrator, a male, on the girl's body and following the trail headed off along the embankment towards Lambeth Bridge, leaving the infuriated detective to his work.

"Never met Sergeant Batty before sir?" asked a constable long familiar with the strange officer's habits, the Inspector merely grunted and watched her striding purposefully towards the river crossing, non-regulation heels clipping on the pavement.

The suspect had made his escape across the bridge, the smell of exhaust fumes was masking his scent and once on the other side of the river the trail died completely, *damn it lost him!*

A second body was reported five minutes later, a man had been found in the small park opposite the Old Boat in Limehouse. Bathory knew the place well, a gay pub on York Square where she and Liz had spent many a happy evening. But before she arrived in her Z3, a new message came in. The headless body of a man had been found on Raby Street only a short distance from York square, Elisabeth gunned the engine she was heading there first.

Bathory studied the decapitated corpse at a distance, SOCO had requested she refrained from contaminating the crime scene but the aroma of garlic was enough to have kept her at arms-length anyway. The hole punched through the chest and the clean cut through the neck was as good as a signature, it was the work of this mysterious spiker. The Ninja had struck again but logic dictated this couldn't be the vampire who had the killed the woman at the memorial, she could just detect human blood over the scent of garlic and knew it would belong to the victim in York Square.

"The killer picked up a human called Daniel Meredith in the pub then took him to the park ostensibly for sex and tore his throat out, very messy. Our spiker caught up with him outside the rope-works a couple of streets away, judging by the smell and the burns around the neck I would say he had been hit with a garlic bomb or something like that before being spiked and decapitated" she had phoned Dee after visiting the crime scene on York Square. "Fingerprints taken from our headless body identified him as a Leo Watts, a petty criminal with a history of violence."

"How did the spiker know there was a vampyr

there?" asked the voice on the other end of the phone.

"I checked with the bar staff, one of them seemed edgy so I checked her name on our database and it appears she worships at St Michael's if you know what I mean?"

"A Watcher?" exclaimed Dee.

"Yes, she reeked of garlic and by the way she was acting I'd say she'd made me as undead."

"This spiker, there's no chance it wasn't the same one?" he asked.

"No, it's this killer from the Low Countries, I'm sure of it, add to this the other death in Westminster and I'd say we had trouble brewing, if this escalates it could damage the Edict, someone's looking for a war!"

"You still think Thurzo is behind this don't you?" asked Dee.

"Who else, I just wish I had killed him all those years ago."

"You have no proof Elisabeth, we must be careful, he is singing the praises of the human killers and some of our brethren are taking notice."

"No proof?" she retorted. "Did you not hear what you just said?"

"I mean to meet with him tomorrow and I would like you to accompany me?"

"Can you trust me not to excise him on the spot?"

"As we will be his guests it would not be seemly, plus he will be well protected."

"I will come with you John I cannot let you walk into danger alone." she ended the call.

CHAPTER SEVENTEEN – THURZO

Whitechapel had in the past been home to a large workhouse, an orphan's asylum (or refuge) and a genuine lunatic asylum going by the grandiose name of The Sir Maundersley Institute for the Mentally Unfortunate. It was nowhere near as big or as infamous as St Mary of Bethlehem, better known as Bedlam, but it served its purpose equally well, hiding away those who *high society* wished to forget. "Maunders" was forced to close in 1897 after a scandal involving the mistreatment of a Marchioness' son and soon fell into rack and ruin. In the early twentieth century, it was purchased by the reclusive G. Thurlow and extensively refurbished as a somewhat eccentric home.

A black Bentley pulled into the yard facing the grim exterior of the building and two figures alighted. "This place is like a fortress," observed Elisabeth taking in the CCTV cameras all around. "Security's bang up to date."

"Well let's get this done." Dee pointed to a large lion-head knocker on the heavy door.

"I'll give you an hour then I'm on the phone to ma

boys and we'll be coming in mob-handed," assured Rob-Roy McGregor who was masquerading as Dee's driver. He shared Bathory's hatred of Thurzo and some of his *clan* of sired vampires were stationed within easy reach of the old asylum, *just to be on the safe side.*

The door was opened by a young-looking vampire wearing a designer dress. "Good evening Sir, Ma'am. Mr Thurzo has been awaiting your arrival."

"She's barely into her teens," whispered Bathory to Dee as they followed the young woman strutting along in her expensive shoes.

"Elisabeth please curb your tongue, we are guests here," replied Dee nervously.

She didn't reply but instead took note of the layout of the ground floor where several thralls were stood around wearing fancy livery. *Renfield could take most of these singlehanded.*

The girl led them into a large room where Thurzo reclined on a throne-like chair with two equally expensively dressed young women at his side.

Bathory found it hard to conceal her contempt, *arrogant bastard, who does he think he is?*

"John, so nice to see you again and you've brought the lovely Erzsebet too." he gestured towards her and addressed his *harem*. "This woman is my dam, she was a formidable vampyr once and without her, you would not have me as your sire." They regarded Bathory and smiled toothily but she was more interested in the group of vampires sat at a nearby table, there were five of them, all male with shaven heads and leather jackets like a quintet of East European gangsters and all looked as though they could handle themselves, they stared at the visitors and Bathory returned the stare.

Thurzo looked disapprovingly at his henchmen. "To what do I owe this pleasure, John?"

"Gyorgy, as you may be aware attacks on humans have increased dramatically over the past couple of weeks.

Given your outburst at the last Executive meeting I wondered if you knew something of the reasons behind them?" asked Dee.

"John, are you insinuating that because I do not find my kindred's willingness to kill for food as disgusting as you, that I am somehow involved?" he countered.

"A bad choice of words perhaps?" asked the elderly vampire. "I will rephrase the question, have you heard anything from any of your acquaintances concerning the growing number of attacks on humans?"

A few of the thuggish types laughed.

"If I had John, rest assured I would not hesitate to tell you."

"Pah!" snorted Elisabeth.

"Erzsebet, the urge to kill lurks inside all of us. I remember the atrocities you committed as a human and if anything, becoming being a vampyr made you a better person."

"I asked Tepesh to turn me into a vampyr. Did any of your young concubines make the same request of you?"

"My esteemed brother and sister may I assure you that I would never turn anyone without their acquiescence," he replied with false sincerity.

"Liar!" snarled Bathory, at this one of Thurzo's brutes came at her, she had anticipated something like this and grabbed his arm twisting it behind his back to hear a satisfying crack followed by a howl of pain then after driving a fist into his face threw her assailant to the ground before stamping one of her high heels into his left eye, the man yelled once again. The rest of the leather jackets stood up and advanced cautiously, half afraid of the elder more experienced vampire. Bathory hissed, taking up an aggressive stance, her face changing, fangs displayed and fingernails now talons.

"You stupid idiot!" shouted Thurzo grabbing the injured man and hauling him to his feet. "You dare attack a guest in my home." he gestured to the others angrily. "You have disgraced my house, leave us alone and take this fool with you.”

“Elisabeth!” exclaimed Dee in horror. Her face had taken on its feral mien, muzzle-like, eyes bright red.

Thurzo’s harem clustered nervously around the big chair. “You go too!” He ordered in less angry tones. “Look at her John, is she not magnificent? Her true nature on display for all to see, it’s in all of us even in one as conciliatory as you. Why should we not give in to the urge to scratch the itch?”

“Never!” replied Dee. “I will not permit what we have achieved to be ruined so easily.”

“You are behind this Georgie, I know you are!” Bathory had regained her human composure.

“So where is your proof, Enforcer?” he retorted.

“I should have killed you all those years ago!”

“But you didn’t! I hold no grudge against you Countess, your desire for revenge made me what I am, you did me the greatest favour possible.”

Dee puffed up angrily. “Gyorgy Thurzo you are openly supporting aggression towards humanity if only indirectly, I summon you to appear before the Executive tomorrow to discuss your future tenure in this country.”

“Ha, do you think I care? Half of them are agreeance with me and with the exception of Erzsebet for whom I hold the greatest respect and that scotch thug McGregor, none of you has the balls to stand up to me and that includes you Doctor Dee, oldest and so-called wisest of our number!”

“Nevertheless you will come to Whitehall tomorrow!” replied Dee, holding his temper in check.

“*Baszd meg regi sodomitadat!*” snarled Thurzo.

“What was that?” asked Dee.

“Ask your *kurva*, she speaks Magyar. Now leave me in peace you old *buzi*!”

“You don’t need to know what he said John, just accept that it wasn’t complimentary” assured Bathory.

They were escorted out by the same young girl while being watched at distance by two of the bald henchmen. One of them was Elisabeth's assailant, his punctured eye already healing.

At the door Bathory spoke quietly to the girl. "How old are you child?"

"Ninety-four, madam," she appeared terrified by her.

"How old were you before you were turned?"

"Sixteen," she whispered almost inaudibly.

"By Thurzo?" asked Bathory, the girl nodded her head. "Did you want it?" the girl shut the door without replying.

"*Fattyu!*" yelled Elisabeth. "John I created a monster!"

"Elisabeth, it seems to me he was already one before you turned him."

CHAPTER EIGHTEEN – RECORDS

"You do realise this is highly irregular and nothing if not inconvenient?" moaned the custodian, not at all happy with the policewoman for interrupting his work.

"But you would still be here wouldn't you?" she countered, *you practically live here*.

"No-one informed me you were coming, is this official business?" asked the man looking at her over his half-moon glasses.

Why does he wear those bloody things, vampyrs don't need them? "Oh come on Talleyrand you know I'm entirely trustworthy."

"I know that every time you come to my department it means trouble!" he snapped.

Henry Talleyrand OBE, had been at the National Archives office for a hundred and fifty years, he'd had to disappear a couple of times to re-emerge with a new identity but since he only worked nights no-one seemed to notice, or care. He was however fanatical about keeping the records up to date.

"Please Henry it is very important," she asked in a ca-joling voice

"Sergeant Bathory, we are re-cataloguing our records and putting them onto the computer, I am very busy and you are keeping me from my work," he said huffily.

"Sooner I get what I need the sooner I'll be gone."

"Hmm, don't know about that?"

"Show me where to look and I will stay out of your hair, promise!"

"Whitechapel was it?"

"Public buildings and utilities in particular," replied Bathory.

The vampire took her to a dim basement and through a maze of corridors to a room full of old filing cabinets. "You'll find what you're looking for in there, we archived these in the sixties, some of the original documents went back as far as Bazalgette's time." he motioned to a com-paratively modern microfiche machine "You can use one of these I take it?"

"I have had some experience with them," she replied sardonically.

With that the custodian of the records office left her to her own devices, it took a couple of hours searching before she finally found what she was looking for.

Bathory smiled and started the printer.

Chapter Nineteen - Emotions

The vampire's head bounced across the floor to land at Renfield's feet. "That was a jolly good blow mistress but I feel we're not going to learn anything from this one now."

Slightly out of breath, Bathory looked from the headless body chained to the wall to Renfield. "The bastard wasn't going to talk anyway," she said by way of explanation, Elisabeth had caught this one drinking the blood pumping from its dying victim's neck. She withdrew her claws as her knuckles, raw from pummelling the captive, slowly began to heal and wiped blackish gore from her face. "Ren, be a darling and pop this thing's head in the furnace, then put it's carcass on the garage roof for the morning sun to deal with."

"Of course mistress and er, may I suggest a shower before meeting with Miss Stride?"

"Renfield, thank you, I will." Her adopted thrall was nearly seven foot in height and built like a tank, he had been a formidable rugby player in the nineteen-twenties before falling foul of a particularly nasty dam called Vita

Cortingen, when Elisabeth excised the vampire she had taken on the giant as her personal assistant, he was loyal to the death and ready to obey any command she issued. Renfield's former mistress was the last elder to publicly refuse to stop killing humans and she had not gone down without a fight as Bathory could attest to. She had to regrow most of her left forearm, one of her lungs and several internal organs after defeating Cortingen and it had required a lot of blood which had been supplied by the Executive in copious amounts, who assured that her no human had died in its acquisition. It was only the second time she had lived up to her gory reputation by lying in a crimson bath as she healed.

Feeling refreshed Elisabeth dressed in a loose robe and came downstairs to find Liz already in the drawing-room, seeing the young woman made her feel warm inside, Liz was lively and funny and Bathory could remember what it felt like to be human in her company "You're not wearing your nurse's outfit tonight?" she asked in mock disappointment.

"No I needed to clean up before I came here and you're not dressed as a policewoman come to that." she observed holding out a blood bag from the hospital "I've brought you a present."

"Oh, you shouldn't have Liz." Bathory joked taking the bag eagerly and cracking the seal to take a deep draft. "Mmm, that's better, I've had a bit of a night my love," the young woman hugged her and Bathory could feel the pulse in her body, it was quite sensual. "Careful, I don't want to spill any." the vampire laughed. "If you don't want me to feed on you just say so, you don't have to bribe me with stolen blood, there's plenty in the fridge."

"I've had a bad night too Beth and I need all the energy I have for what I've got planned."

"Really?" asked Bathory with a smile.

"Really!" grinned Liz making a scissoring action with her fingers before slipping the robe from the vampire's unresisting shoulders.

***

"I think I should have taken some blood just to slow you down a bit." Elisabeth joked later, she began kissing Liz's neck then ran her tongue from shoulder to jaw. "I can feel the pulse in your carotid, it's very arousing."

Liz looked at her. "Your fangs are down, you promised you wouldn't?" she scolded.

Bathory shrugged and with some effort retracted her canines. "Why do you stay with me when you know how dangerous I am?"

"Because the danger turns me on… and I really like you, Beth," she replied. "I like you a lot."

"Despite all the terrible things I've done?"

Liz put her head on Elisabeth's pale breast. "I don't believe everything that's written about you."

"Some of it is exaggerated but I did do a lot of harm, I killed…"

Liz put a finger on the vampire's lips. "I don't want to know, tell me about your night instead."

"Not a good idea, tell me about your night first, no matter how bad it was."

"We had someone brought in with terrible lacerations to the neck, we tried our best but they'd lost so much blood, the throat had been ripped open."

"It looks like your night and mine might have crossed over, I caught a vampyr in the act and dragged it back here for interrogation."

She sat up suddenly. "You didn't stay to help the victim?"

"Sorry, I did call the human police anonymously."

"Did you excise it?"

"Yes, I er, well the bloody thing wouldn't talk, I lost my temper and knocked its head off."

"Ugh, I almost wish I hadn't asked."

"I'm sorry I didn't try to save that bloke."

"Bloke?" asked Liz.

"The one who had his throat ripped open?"

"Nada, it was a woman."

"Oh no, what time was she brought in?"

"Ten to two this morning, just before I was supposed to come off shift," replied Liz.

Bathory had intercepted the vampire at least an hour earlier so he couldn't have been the culprit, *oh bollocks, why*

CHAPTER TWENTY - WATCHERS

Tina swung the sabre to deliver the coup de grace, acting upon a tip-off from the Watcher community she had wandered around Soho with the Oculus concealed in her hand using it on suspicious-looking individuals until finally she had spotted the creature lurking in the shadows on Berwick Street where a lot of renovation work was going on, *probably hoping to pick off a punter emerging from the nearby burlesque club*. Driving the spike in before it had chance to react, she dragged the vampire into a yard to finish the excision then after putting the severed head into a canvas bag, went through its pockets to discover it had been Zander Hope, only twenty years old or had been. The vampire was newly turned and inexperienced, the second such she had excised in three days. Christiana walked out of the alley hoping the coming morn would shine enough light on the carcass to immolate it before it could be discovered. The Watchers were feeding her information about local vampires but had yet to supply anything regarding her quarry, *were they stringing her along hoping she would thin out the local undead for them, they had better bloody well not be!*

Arriving at St Michael's next morning she threw the canvas bag to a beefy looking verger. "Furnace for that and don't bother opening it, it's from last night and it might be a bit ripe" she suggested before asking. "Is Father Gervase about?"

The man silently pointed to a door and she entered his office. "Ah Christiana, I was hoping you would arrive soon, good night's hunting was it?"

"I found and excised the creature as you asked, so, do you have anything of more interest for me?"

Gervase looked at the woman. She was maybe thirty with blue eyes and mousey hair, athletically built and quite pleasant looking. "I have the whereabouts of your quarry, but first I need you to do me one more favour, another excision."

"Of course you do," replied Tina sardonically. "This has to be the last one then you give me Thurlow, agreed?"

"Yes, I swear in the name of our Lord that this will be the last and then I'll give you his location, I'll even detail some of our converts to assist you."

"Good, so where is this creature you want me to excise?"

CHAPTER TWENTY-ONE - CONFRONTATION

Liz parked her car and after taking her shopping out of the back, made her way up the stairs to the front door, as she opened it someone pushed her into the apartment clasping a hand around her mouth and twisting her arm behind her back. "Be quiet and you won't get hurt! I'm not here for you just your mistress."

Liz instead bit the hand as hard as she could and wresting herself free screamed at the top of her voice. "Beth, Beth, wake up!"

"Fucking bitch!" snarled Christiana knocking the nurse to the floor then upon hearing a noise turned to see a naked form charging at her from the bedroom, the front door had swung shut behind her and the room was in half-darkness. *Fuck it!*

Knocking aside the black torch before she had time to use it, Bathory grabbed Tina and threw her against the wall, pinning her there with one hand. "The Ninja I presume, now I want to know just one thing before I kill you, are you a fucking Van Helsing?"

"Yes, bitch!" Christina bit hard on the false tooth

she'd had fitted especially for the purpose and blew a cloud of garlic vapour into Elisabeth's eyes, as the vampire cried in pain Tina hooked her ankle with a foot and pushing hard sent Bathory backwards. She landed on her back where she lay winded as Van Helsing jumped onto her and pushed a spike into her chest.

Bathory blinded, now found she couldn't move, the impalement had rendered her immobile and in indescribable pain, she struggled to speak but was unable to so.

Christina watched as the vampire's eyes, milky white from the searing garlic, began to heal, the colour of her irises slowly reappearing, she withdrew the spike slightly to ask mockingly. "So, who are you then?"

"Go and fuck yourself!" Bathory replied with difficulty through gritted teeth.

She pushed the spike back in to a fresh howl from the vampire and twisted it so the corners of its star-shaped blade caused greater pain, after withdrawing it once more Christiana asked. "We'll try again, who are you? Tell me or this is going straight through to your backbone!"

"Elisabeth Bathory of Ecsedi." she gasped, the point was scraping on her heart.

"Well, I'll be b…" Tina didn't finish as Liz, who had regained her senses barrelled into her and the spike, still clutched in the hunter's hand came free of Bathory's chest as the two women wrestled briefly for control of the weapon. Tina, being the more experienced fighter quickly gained the upper hand and hauling Liz to her feet, pushed the spike against her throat as the vampire slowly and painfully stood. "Countess fucking Blood!" snarled Christiana. "How many innocent people did you kill, fifty, or was it three hundred?"

"It's all lies, tell her it's not true Beth!" cried Liz.

"Come on *Beth*, tell your little pet the truth" sneered Tina.

"Let her go and I will kill you quickly and mercifully but if you harm a hair on her head I can promise you a painful lingering death, you would do well to remember my reputation spiker!" Bathory's voice had taken on a strange timbre, the whites of her healed eyes had changed to blood red, her upper and lower canines were fully extended and her face had extended to take on an animalistic appearance.

"Look at your mistress and see her as she truly is!" Christiana had excised many undead but this was the first elder she had encountered and it was terrifying to behold.

"She is not a pet she is my friend, now let her go now!" growled a feral Bathory.

"Tell her how you bathed in maidens blood, do it creature!" shouted Tina pressing the point of the spike against the nurse's neck, a tiny trickle of blood appeared.

"Only once did I do such a thing, I had fought a newly turned Turk who was terrorising the land, I excised him but was badly injured doing so and needed to heal" answered the vampire, concern for her partner showing on the terrible visage.

"See, she was protecting the humans, Beth's not that bad," exclaimed Liz.

"You were just guarding your flock weren't you?" suggested Tina. "Didn't want anyone else raiding the pantry?"

"Yes," replied Bathory resignedly.

"No!" cried Liz.

"They were criminals! The only woman among them killed her children to enable her marriage to a rich man, they were all due to be executed so why not put them to good use?"

"No." repeated Liz quietly.

"I'm sorry my darling, I told you I was dangerous" she looked at Van Helsing and said calmly. "Just let her go unharmed and I give you my word I won't attack you."

"Why should I believe you?" asked Tina.

"I will let you recover your black lamp, if I move you can use it on me."

Christiana released the nurse who unexpectedly kicked the torch out of reach before rushing to Bathory's side. The hunter held out the spike expecting the creature to charge, *if only I'd worn my sword*, it was in her sports bag next to the front door. Palming a garlic bomb from the bandolier she spotted a small gap in the curtains allowing a chink of daylight through *if I could just get to the window...*

"Well, what now spiker?" asked the vampire resuming her human form, she had wrapped a protective arm around the young woman who was examining the wound under her breast.

"Are you a policewoman, or is that just a sham?" *she must delay the creature.*

She gave a thin smile. "People have asked me that a lot recently. I keep watch on my own kind to prevent them from killing humans. I protect your people under the Edict."

"While taking their blood as payment, correct?" asked Tina.

"The Edict forbids killing but keeping the peace has a price."

"I would say that's not working out too well." *if she could just edge to the window.* "So what happened to make Countess Dracula so altruistic?"

"Years of pain, a couple of selfless acts by humans coupled with overwhelming guilt at what I had done, I have had a lot of time to rethink my unlife and have spent much of it trying to atone for my crimes." Bathory saw Christiana glancing towards the curtains. "Don't bother, I would get there before you could, I gave you my word spiker I will not kill you today but I cannot guarantee it should we meet again. Why did you come here Van Helsing's spawn, are there no vampyrs left in Europe to excise?"

"I am looking for one, in particular, a Georgie Thurlow."

"Really, so why did you come after me?"

"A certain group has information regarding Thurlow's whereabouts. They said if I were to excise the police vampiress they would tell me where to find the other creature."

"Fasz!" exclaimed Elisabeth. "That'll be the bloody Watchers, you are a fool, do you not realise they're using you to foment trouble between human and vampyr? As an elder I am both feared and respected by the younger kin but with me gone many would feel emboldened to kill, to say nothing of the lust for revenge that would grow in the hearts of my fellow elders over my excision."

"Really and how would that help the Watchers?" she sneered.

"Very few people take them seriously, they desperately want to expose our existence to the world and if they succeed there would be armies of human soldiers wearing bite-proof armour armed with garlic coated bullets and ultra-violet lamps. We would be hunted to extinction."

"You're asking me to care about that? I'd exterminate the bloody lot of you tomorrow!" retorted Tina.

"We wouldn't down go without a fight, spiker, it would be carnage, we own the night remember?"

Christiana thought on her words, *a world without vampires but at what cost?* "I just need to know where this bastard lives then once I've excised it, I'll go back to Amsterdam. It's a matter of family honour."

"I know the vampyr you are seeking and he will make for a very dangerous foe."

"The Watchers promised their help if I excised you."

"Go tell them you have succeeded and I will keep a low profile until you are done, one way or the other."

"Why are you doing this?"

"I have my reasons, now go before I change my mind, spiker!"

As Bathory dressed in the bedroom she heard the front door open and close then re-joined Liz to remark. "She's almost certainly going to her to death."

"Can't you do something Beth?"

"Van Helsing came here to destroy me, why should I?"

"And yet you let her go unharmed, you are a far better person than the Blood Countess ever was."

Bathory thought for a moment, she had a grudging respect for the brave woman who had fought so valiantly. "I'm going to see Dee the minute the sun goes down and you're going to call in sick and start packing, right now!"

"What?"

"You need to go to your mother's in Yorkshire and stay there, things might turn very nasty very soon and I don't want you in harm's way."

CHAPTER TWENTY-TWO - BURNED

Christiana sat on the tube feeling uneasy, she had backed away from excising one of the most famous vampires in history, Elisabeth Bathory was second only in infamy to Vlad Tepesh, *was she going soft? Don't kid yourself, she let you go,* she would need backup to go against her again. *Don't call it her, they are creatures nothing more!* Yet Bathory had a companion who she clearly showed affection for *and was willing to let me go, even if it was only to trick the Watchers? Why was the creature so amenable, had she really reformed over the centuries?*

Christiana could hear the sirens as she emerged from Farringdon station, it was only a short walk to St Michael's from here and in the other direction lay the old meat market where she had first encountered Bathory. As she made her way along Saffron Hill the acrid smell of smoke assaulted her nostrils and she could see flashing blue lights in the distance and drawing closer Christiana could see the Victorian church aflame with the fire brigade playing hoses on the blaze. The fire was brought under control quite quickly and Christiana attempted to get closer only to be stopped at the cordon by a policeman who was unable to give her any information about her *Uncle Gervase,* the priest there.

While standing in the crowd of onlookers a hand fell on her shoulder and with a start she turned to see a nun who Christiana recognised as one of the Watchers. "Are you alright Sister Margaret?"

"Yes thank you, child, the good Lord saw fit to let me escape unharmed but they've taken the Reverend Father, they burst in all dressed in black and knocked down Mr Briggs, the Father told me to run as they grabbed him and I called the police but when I came back the place was on fire, may God smite them all down!"

"They attacked the church in broad daylight? Asked Christiana, *they had to have been thralls!*

"Yes, Miss Van Helsing, I know what you're thinking, these people weren't the undead but their damned and godless followers." They watched as firemen entered the smouldering ruin with an empty body bag. "Poor Mr Briggs, God rest his soul."

***

Dee sat feeling stunned on the comfortable settee in his lavishly furnished room, the civil servant stood before him flanked by two tough-looking men in military uniform, each wore body armour that protected their necks and as well as the automatic rifles they carried each had a large pistol grip torch hung at their belts, he didn't have to ask to know they were ultra-violet lamps and all three humans reeked nauseatingly of garlic. As the enormity of what he had been told sank in he muttered. "The Watcher's church is destroyed?"

"The shell of it still stands and the fire brigade has recovered what was left of the verger, a man called Briggs. Early forensic reports suggest petrol was used as an accelerant," explained the bureaucrat.

"It couldn't have been done by the brethren, not in the daytime!" it was still only mid-afternoon, one of his thralls had woken him from slumber after the civil servant had hammered on the door demanding to be let in. Both now stood defensively behind their seated master.

"But many of you have slaves to do your bidding don't you?" the man replied coldly regarding the two muscular young men.

"Are you insinuating I'm behind this?" asked Dee angrily.

"No of course not, like me, you prefer to have these Watchers around as useful idiots but whoever did this went a step too far. Someone in your damnable community is stirring up trouble so what are you going to do about it, Doctor Dee?"

"I have brought in help from other regions, London will be well protected tonight I can assure you. We will discover who is behind this and bring an end to it."

The bureaucrat smiled mirthlessly. "You have one week Doctor, we have been observing your kind for a while and we know where a great many of you, what is the correct term, un-live?"

"No doubt they will all be those brethren who exist peacefully alongside humans and if you persecute those who follow the Edict, who will enforce it on those who hide from you?" asked Dee.

"There will be black streetlamps installed around the city, garlic sprays will be standard issue for all police officers and of course these gentlemen with me are merely part of a much larger force being trained to be deployed as necessary. We tolerate your kind at the moment but this could all change so easily." As the Secretary made to leave he turned to say. "One week Dee, bear that in mind."

***

Christiana sat in a pub not far from her hotel looking at the empty schnapps glass in front of her, *getting drunk isn't going to help*. She had failed to excise a notorious vampire and her main contact in London was by now either dead or turned, her crusade for revenge was failing and her spirits with it, when night fell she would make one last sortie around Whitechapel and return to Amsterdam tomorrow.

As dusk fell she picked up her battered sports bag and went out onto the streets in the forlorn hope of finding a creature who might know where to find Thurlow while elsewhere, Bathory, now reinforced by McGregor and a dozen of his vampyr clan sallied forth into the night, grimly determined to keep the humans safe at all costs.

CHAPTER TWENTY-THREE
- ABIGAIL

It had been a long night but between them, Bathory and McGregor had caught at least a dozen new turn-ees but disturbing reports on her police radio told of three murders that bore all the hallmarks of blood rage and worse, Dee had informed her that his Civil Service contact was making renewed threats about deploying the special-forces response unit.

Bathory was driving to her partner's flat. Liz, reluctant to desert her post was finally leaving for Yorkshire tomorrow and although unable to accompany her to the railway station in daylight she would at least feel happier in the knowledge the nurse had got off safely. The Watcher's HQ had been burned down but if there was an afterlife, the vampire could imagine Father Gervase would no doubt be laughing at them in heaven.

Her mobile rang, it was Harker. "Elisabeth, I've caught a bloody vampire in my flat!"

"What?" she exclaimed. "What do you mean caught it?"

"Pinned it to the floor with a kitchen knife and it's not

dead yet."

"You'll need to decapitate it," stated Bathory, as if it was the most normal thing in the world.

"Whaat?" he cried. "Sarge I can't do that, I called you for help."

"It'll be daylight soon and I need to be somewhere else before then."

"Elisabeth, this has got something to do with you I know it has! I didn't even believe in vampires until the other night, please it's making horrible noises, Sarge, you owe me!"

She looked at the car clock. "Dammit James, I have plans."

"And I have a fucking vampire stuck to my living room floor!" he shouted.

"I'll be there in twenty minutes, make sure all the curtains are shut and get ready to let me in quickly!" she would ring Liz when she got up.

Bathory managed to park her black BMW quite close to Harker's ground floor flat and rushed up the front steps just as the sun appeared over the building.

As he shut the door behind her Bathory announced angrily. "Well, that's me stuck here all day!" then she saw the young woman lying flat on her back, she was dressed in jeans and t-shirt and the handle of a carving knife was sticking out of her chest, she was also making mewling noises and twitching her limbs feebly. "You've made a fucking bad job of that!" Bathory informed him.

"Well yeah, I guess I missed the vampire-slaying lecture during training! Elisabeth, the fucking thing was already here in my flat when I came off shift, she tried to bite me but shied away when she got near, I guess it was something to do with the garlic sausage sandwich I ate earlier, we wrestled, I grabbed a knife from the worktop and...." he gestured to the floor.

"Garlic sausage, what have I told you about bloody garlic?" snapped Bathory.

"Well, I didn't expect to be seeing you today and anyway it saved my life!" he retorted.

Bathory grunted in acknowledgement and straddled the impaled vampire to stare into the wild eyes. "This must be hurting you a lot so I'm going to pull it out *and* you're going be a good little girl and stay where you are." As she withdrew the knife the newly turned vampire snarled and lunged upward, fangs extended. Bathory's visage changed, her jaw lengthened, the front of her face moved forward flattening her nose and she bared sharp elongated upper and lower canines. "Don't you try it on with me girl, I'm older than you and far more dangerous." she hissed.

The younger woman shrank back submissively. "Bloody Hell Sarge, I've never seen you do that before!" exclaimed Harker, *she looks like a bat!*

Bathory's countenance returned to its normal striking appearance. "You've never made me that angry James."

"Please don't kill me" whimpered the girl pinned under Bathory's silk-clad legs, she had an American accent.

"She needs blood," stated Bathory looking at Harker.

"No fucking way!" he retorted emphatically, backing away slightly.

She looked in askance and tossed her car keys to him. "In the boot of my car there's a cool box, fetch it for me and when you go out only open the front door as much as you need to, the sun's shining straight down this street now." after he had left she turned to her captive. "So missy, tell me how you got this way and no more funny business.

"I was at a cocktail bar in Piccadilly with some friends and when I went out back to go to the bathroom someone grabbed me in the yard. I woke up in a room with tiles all over it and there was a strange taste in my mouth. I lay there for hours and I was so hungry but all I could think about was blood, then someone came into the room and gave me this cup and it tasted metallic and I realised I was drinking blood and it was so disgusting and yet I wanted more." Her face fell. "Oh god, I'm a vampire aren't I?"

"Yes, you were given vampyr blood while you were semi-conscious and that explains the taste in your mouth. Sorry, my dear but you've been turned and that cup was your first meal of human blood." Bathory informed her sympathetically. A blinding wash of light came into the room as James came back inside and the young woman stared at him hungrily. As he put the container down next to them, she hissed, reaching towards him with a clawed hand. Knocking it aside Elisabeth took out a blood bag and asked. "Now do you have a name?"

"Abigail," she replied.

"Right Abigail let's get this clear straight away, my friend James is not on the menu. Now tell me, do you have any idea who did this to you?"

"I don't know, they always wore hoods and I was blindfolded when they brought me here."

"You were brought here?" exclaimed Harker in surprise.

"Yes, they told me I could have all the blood I wanted I just had to take it from you."

"Who told you to do that?" demanded Bathory.

"I don't know, give me that bag, I need it!" she cried snatching at the blood pouch.

Bathory held it away. "You're like me now, all your senses are enhanced did you hear or smell anything?"

"No… wait, there was a man who had an accent like yours and he spoke to someone in a strange language," Bathory asked her the question again in Hungarian. "That's it, he spoke just like that." Elisabeth gave Abigail the blood bag and she grabbed it to begin drinking noisily.

"It was that bastard Thurzo!" she exclaimed.

"The one who had you walled up?" asked James.

"Yes him, he must have had people watching you…" her voice trailed off. *If they were watching James they would doubtless be watching Liz as well.*

Shakily, she rang the nurse's phone and was relieved

when it was answered. "Hi darling, why aren't you home?" she asked.

"Sorry my love there's been an emergency and now I'm stuck at a colleague's place. You're all packed and ready aren't you?"

"Yes, mother." She replied in a mocking voice.

"I'm worried that's all, I'll get Renfield to escort you to the station."

"Don't be fucking stupid, Beth, it's broad daylight outside I'll be perfectly safe."

"Look, just be careful!"

"Yes mummy, love you, mummy," said Liz lightly.

"Sod off to Wakefield you stupid bitch." laughed Bathory hanging up. She looked up to see James and Abigail staring at her, she shrugged and passed the new vampire another blood pouch. "Right prom queen, make yourself at home and don't forget you'll fry if you go outside." she smiled at Harker grabbing his collar. "You... bedroom, if I'm stuck here all day I need to pass the time somehow."

"But wasn't that your girlfriend?" asked the policeman.

"Shut up and get in there, Abi if you disturb us for anything other than an unlife threatening situation I will spike you properly!"

Bathory lay in Harker's bed staring at the ceiling and unable to sleep, their lovemaking had been satisfying but she couldn't get Liz out of her mind, the policeman started to snore and she turned his head away. *Damn it James I thought screwing you would prevent me from loving Liz, all it's doing is making me feel guilty.*

She slipped on her uniform shirt which was just long enough to cover her decency and wandered into the sitting room, the girl was huddled on the settee watching the television.

"Can't sleep either huh?" asked Bathory

"I've just watched my parents on the news begging

me to contact them, apparently I disappeared three days ago" her face was tear-stained. "My life is screwed isn't it?"

"I'm sorry, your human life is over but you have a long future as a vampyr ahead of you."

"Mom and dad, my friends, family, I can't see them again can I?"

"It would be difficult, not impossible perhaps."

"What am I going to do?" she was close to tears again.

Bathory sat down and put her arm around the girl. "You'll get used to it and make new undead friends and there are sympathetic humans too. You can stay at my house until you're sorted, there are plenty of spare rooms" *I don't know what Liz is going to think… Liz…*

"Why are you being so nice, I just tried to kill your boyfriend?"

"Because I can't bear to see you on your own at such a dreadful time and he's not my boyfriend, we have sex that's all," *that's because you already have a girlfriend who you love* said a voice in her head.

"And a girlfriend too?" asked Abi.

"Yes!" *who I love… stop it Bathory!*

"Elisabeth I'm hungry but I don't want blood, can I still eat normal food?"

"Yes, as long as you remember that garlic is now like sulfuric acid to you."

"You lead quite a life," remarked Abi rummaging through Harker's cupboard to find a box of cornflakes.

"We generally refer to it as an unlife." Bathory absentmindedly passed her a bottle of milk from the fridge then a feeling of unease came over her and she went to find her phone and ring Liz, there was no answer so she shook the sleeping policeman. "James, wake up, I'm worried and I need your help."

She stood in shadow inside the open front door staring at the glaring daylight, Harker had mounted the car on the pavement and the passenger door was wide open.

"Elisabeth there's no-one about, if you're doing to this, now would be a good time," he called.

"That's easy for you to say, James, you try running through a furnace!" she could see him shimmering in an ultraviolet haze visible only to a vampire.

"Elisabeth!" he yelled.

"*O, fasz!*" pulling the blanket over her head she ran out into the blistering sun and dived into the car as Harker shut the door behind her.

He closed the door to his flat after shouting to Abi it would be safe to come out of the bedroom then quickly jumped into the UV protected car to see Bathory hiding under the thick blanket. "Driver's door is shut you can come out now."

Bathory lowered the blanket looking a tourist who had forgotten the sun lotion then began painfully peeling strips of melted silk from her boiled ham legs. "Stupid *kurva*, why did I put my bloody stockings on?" she asked aloud.

"Will you be okay?" he could smell burnt flesh.

"Yes, give me some blood!"

Harker passed over a pouch from the box in the back of the car which Bathory gratefully took and asked. "Did you leave enough for Abi?"

"Yes Sarge, in the fridge, so where does this Liz Stride live then?"

***

Bathory had nearly recovered when they arrived at the nurse's apartment but the flat was on the first floor and even though the street was in the shade, Harker insisted on going instead of her. Elisabeth was examining her legs which were still quite pink when Harker got back into the car. "Did you find anything?" she asked concerned.

"The place is tidy, no sign of a struggle and I couldn't find her case on top of the wardrobe."

"Did you find the pink rucksack with unicorns on it?"

"No Sarge, it looks like she got off alright."

"Then why isn't she answering her phone?"

"She could have forgotten to charge it or perhaps she's in one of those carriages that don't let you get a signal?" suggested Harker.

"Maybe, James, I need one more favour. I can't get through to Renfield either, drive me home."

CHAPTER TWENTY-FOUR
- BLOODBATH

Harker drove the BMW straight into the garage and curiously the door was open, concerned that it might be broken, Elisabeth used her phone to remotely operate it and was relieved to see it close shutting off the dangerous daylight. *Why had Renfield left it open, he knew better than that?* As she got out of the car the smell of blood was overpowering, it was from a vampire but there the scent of human was mixed in with it.

"Is that what I think it is?" asked the young policeman regarding the gory puddle.

She nodded. "It came from one of my kind!"

Ordering Harker to stay put, Bathory cautiously entered the corridor leading from the garage to follow the trail of blood through the kitchen and into the hall to discover Renfield's disembowelled body at the foot at the stairs. She closed his staring eyes while taking note of the hand-axe still held in his dead fingers, dark blood was still sticky on the blade and a nail-gun converted to fire short spikes lay nearby. *At least he took some of the bastards with him!* Judging by the amount of undead blood splashed around she estimated that at least two vampyrs had met their fate at his hands and there was a lot of human blood too, not all of it Renfield's.

Going back to the kitchen, she watched the CCTV footage showing a van with its windows blacked out approach the house to pause for a half a minute before heading out of shot and presumably into the garage, *they must have hacked the door circuit, Thurzo had to be behind this!*

"Fucking hell!" cried Harker upon spotting the mutilated body in the hall. Tired of waiting he had come into the kitchen. "I think I'm going to be sick."

"The toilet's the way you came in, if you must vomit please do it there." she sat back and was about to call Dee when Harker motioned urgently to her. On the floor near the kitchen door was a familiar backpack, it was pink with unicorns all over it.

Bathory rushed back to the hallway where Renfield's eviscerated corpse lay to carefully sniff at the air, Liz's scent was all over the house as a matter of course and she hadn't considered that the nurse might still be here. Bathory felt a cold feeling in the pit of her stomach as she realised the scent was fresher than a day old and following it upstairs ran to the main bedroom to throw open the door terrified of what she might find, the room appeared to be empty but the smell of Liz' blood was overpowering.

At the foot of Elisabeth's four-poster bed was a large trunk used as a blanket chest, the contents were strewn about the room and the lid wasn't quite closed, she had once joked it was big enough for a body but neither Bathory with her long legs or the shorter Liz could fit themselves in. She opened the chest in great trepidation to discover Liz clad only in underwear with her limbs broken to fit her inside.

Harker, who had followed, just stood speechless as Bathory howled in anguish. "I will tear Thurzo's heart out, I will flay his skin and give his worthless body to the sunlight!" the vampire spat, her countenance becoming feral once more.

There was a slight noise from the trunk and Harker felt for a pulse, after some difficulty he found it, weak and erratic. "Elisabeth, she's still alive!"

Tearing the chest apart as though it was made of matchwood Bathory gently lifted the limp broken form out of the wreckage and placed her on the mattress noticing she was covered in bite-marks. As she gently bent the nurse's twisted limbs to approximately the right shape she arched her body and moaned before falling back to the bed motionless.

The policeman felt for her pulse again and it was barely there, she was dying. "I'll phone for an ambulance."

"No, no, no!" cried Bathory, she knew what had to be done and tearing at her wrist with talon-like fingernails let a few small drops of dark blood fall on the young woman's black-painted lips. There was no reaction so she opened Liz's mouth and clenched her fist to force a stream of the dark fluid into it from the wound. "Take it, my love, please take it!" she raised Liz's head slightly to allow the vampire blood to run into her stomach and as it seeped into her internal organs she began to shudder then an awful scream came from her lungs. Bathory kissed her on the forehead. "I'm so sorry Liz, I had to turn you, you will heal but it's going to hurt a lot." she looked at the constable. "James, she's going to need a lot of blood, there are pouches in the fridge and the garage freezer, bring them all here now!"

The intruders had stolen the supply from the fridge but fortunately, the cache in the garage had not been discovered. As Harker rushed upstairs with his arms full of frozen blood a fresh scream of pain came from above, as he entered the bedroom Elisabeth snatched a pouch from him and tore it open to squeeze some of the frozen mush into Liz's mouth. The newly created vampire swallowed it frantically, almost unaware of what she was doing and Harker watched in astonishment as the bites faded and the twisted limbs slowly began to straighten, the tenting of the skin where the broken ends of bones protruded became shallower, flattening out and smoothing.

Bathory popped a bag under her armpit to hasten its defrosting then fed Liz the rest of the red slush from the open pouch. Her eyelids flickered open briefly. "Beth… Renfield, they killed him…"

"Shh, he was very brave and you need to heal, don't waste your strength."

Liz clutched at her with her undamaged hand. "It hurts, Beth, don't leave me alone."

"I won't until you're better." *Then, I'm going to tear Thurzo's heart out.*

After Elisabeth had sent Harker to check on Abi, she laid the bags on the floor to count them, estimating there to be just enough to get her partner through this with one spare, she cracked the seal on the partially defrosted bag and drank the cold liquid, she would have it preferred it warmer but it would have to do.

Liz woke later with a cry and Bathory fed her more blood. "You got your wish Beth, I'm never going to be able to go out in the sun again am I?" she asked with red-stained lips.

"No Liz, I would give anything for this not to have happened, but now we can be together forever."

"Promise?" she asked weakly.

"Yes, I love you, Liz Stride. I've been afraid to get too close but now I can let my heart rule my head, how are your arms and legs?"

"Very painful," she whispered.

"So much that I can't hold you?" asked the vampire.

"I'd like that."

Bathory took off her shoes and got on the bed taking Liz gently in her arms, pulling the covers over them as she did.

"You didn't have to do that I'm not cold… is that part of being a vampire?"

"External conditions won't affect you how they used

to, how's your sense of smell?"

"I can smell your scent, it's nice."

"You'll be able to see in the dark now, you're going to be so much stronger and faster soon and have all the other traits of vampirism."

Liz drifted back into unconsciousness then woke again after an hour to ask. "Will I have to bite people?" she still didn't much relish the idea.

"You'll find it hard to stop yourself when the blood calls to you," answered Bathory.

"Talking of which I really would like some more," she confessed, her canines were becoming pointed.

She held another blood bag to the newly undead woman's lips watching her greedily devour it, *another mouth to feed!*

Liz regained enough strength to relate that she had arrived early for the train and was waiting on the platform when a message came on the tannoy that she was to meet a Mr Renfield at the information desk. Thinking Bathory had sent him to check on her she had set off but didn't arrive, someone bumped into her and everything went black, the nurse had begun to regain her wits as they arrived at Bathory's house to see that Renfield was already dead and she had been fully conscious when they worked on her to fit her into the trunk.

Dee sent a sanitation team to deal with the body and clear up the mess made during the mêlée, he also sent for Gretchen Piggott, a "sitter" who arrived as dusk fell with a fresh batch of blood. She would nurse Liz through the final stage of transition while Bathory was necessarily absent.

The phone rang and it was the Doctor himself. "Elisabeth, this must be awful for you, has Gretchen arrived?"

"Yes, she's with Liz. You do know it was Thurzo don't you?"

"You can't be sure of that?"

"What they did to Liz was a parody of what he did to me all those years ago, the bastard may as well have signed his name to it."

"Elisabeth!"

"I'm not joining you tonight John, I'm going to Whitechapel and I'm going to make him suffer before I excise him!"

"No, you mustn't, think of the consequences, you're putting yourself in great danger!"

"I don't fucking care, Thurzo will pay for what he has done!"

"You saw his lair, it's a fortress." cried Dee.

"I've already found a way in John, one I'll bet he doesn't know about."

"Stay there I'm coming round."

"I won't be here." she slammed the phone down and turned to the kindly old vampire sat by the bed. "Gretchen, when Liz wakes up, remind her that I love her and when Dee arrives tell him it's too late and if this sparks a war then so be it."

Bathory went into the garage and entered a code into the keypad belonging to a large metal cupboard and opening the door put on a stab vest over the police riot coverall she was already wearing. Buckling a sheathed *parang* around her waist she selected another converted nail driver from the shelf, as a weapon it had little range and accuracy but it was useful at close quarters and she intended to get very close to her foe.

Thus prepared Elisabeth removed the cover from a large powerful motorbike, donned a black-visored helmet and started the engine. Then with a roar from her motorised steed she rode out into the darkness with revenge in her heart.

Chapter Twenty-five - Captive

A deluge of freezing water brought Christiana Van Helsing back to the world. She was lying naked on a cold floor and upon opening blurry eyes could make out white tiles, everywhere hurt.

"Nice of you to join us Miss Van Helsing or might I call you Christiana?" said a voice.

"*Fuck op!*" she muttered.

"Ah, so it's the same in Dutch as it is in English." continued the voice. "Sorry about the state of your accommodation but we have had to wait for you to piss that garlic away."

She had been taken captive outside her hotel in broad daylight by a pair of burly men and bundled into the back of a van to be driven to… *where?* After receiving a beating and an intimate search they had thrown her into this cold tiled room, it was her habit to consume plenty of garlic-laden food when in *bandit country* and upon realising this her abductors had been forcing water down her to flush the poisonous herb from her system. Christiana had tried to hang on as long as possible but nature had eventually taken its course.

Someone jabbed a needle in her arm to withdraw blood and she looked up to hazily see a grim-faced woman squirting a syringe into a small bowl, as her vision came into focus she saw a tall man with an impressive moustache watching the proceedings curiously. He gestured to a nervous young vampire who tentatively dipped her finger in and licked it.

"Not enough Tamsin, drink it all." ordered the man, she drained the bowl then nodded licking her lips.

"Excellent, poor Tamsin has been quite sick several times today so I imagine you must be free of the bloody stuff now. You've had a good run spiker but your time has come to an end, so tell me, why do you want me excised?"

"You're Thurlow?" *how does he know I'm after him?*

"Thurlow?" he laughed. "That's what they call me, yes. So what do you want?"

"Go fuck yourself, undead scum!" she spat, *if I'm going to die, why should I satisfy his curiosity?*

"Suit yourself, Miss Van Helsing I was merely being curious."

"Why am I still alive, are you planning on turning me because if you did I'd go out in the sun the first chance I got?" spat Christiana defiantly.

"You would perhaps feel differently if I did, but no, I'm having a get-together tonight and you're the guest of honour, or perhaps I should say the main course! We even have dessert in the form of an old friend of yours" he grinned then turning to a burly man stood at the door said. "Oz, take the bitch to the cell and Tamsin, fetch her clothes so she can have some dignity back for the remainder of her short life."

Christiana was thrown into a dark room with her things, as she sat on a hard bench to dress a slight groan caught her ear and as her eyes adjusted to the dim light she could see a huddled shape in the corner of the room. "Hello?" she called.

"Is that you Christiana?" asked a wavering voice.

"Father Gervase, you're still alive?"

"Yes my dear girl, though I wish it were otherwise."

"While we live there's hope Father." *And that's about it really.*

"Did Sister Margaret escape?"

"Yes, Father but I'm afraid Mr Briggs didn't."

"Poor Simon, he was a devout and true believer *and* a good strong arm when the Lord required it."

"How did they know who I was Father?" asked Tina accusingly.

"It's my fault, Christiana, I betrayed you to them may God forgive me. They threatened me with great pain and I am a weak man, I told them whatever they wanted to know including the identity of the spiker from the lowlands."

"Yeah well, I don't know how well I'd cope under torture, Father," she said with a sympathy she didn't feel. "We have to find a way out of here." *attack the guard when he comes in? need a weapon for that,* she felt along the walls trying to find a nail or loose stone or anything but there was nothing she could use, they had even taken the wires from her bra *if there was only one guard perhaps she could strangle him with it? Plan 38b,* she smiled grimly, *it was almost funny.*

A thin shaft of light coming through the tiny window at the top of the wall was dimming perceptibly. "It'll be dark soon then they'll come for us. Give us strength Lord!" cried the priest in a quavering tone.

***

Christiana had no idea how long she had sat miserably in the dark while Father Gervase still huddled in the corner, kept repeating the same passages from the bible over and again when a noise came from outside.

"Showtime!" came the gruff tones of one of Thurlow's goons and she recognised it as belonging to the one who had been rather free with his hands when she was being searched. Then another voice was heard, *there were at least two of them out there, that's plan 38B gone out of the window!*

The lock began to turn. *Oh, god this is it!* Christiana stood, determined to put up a fight and hoping she could be defiant until the end, but the Father however, collapsed into blubbering and begging the Lord for forgiveness.

There was the sound of a scuffle followed by a cry that cut off sharply then the door swung slowly open to reveal a vampire in feral mode, blood dripping from its chin. "Well spiker, you are in a pickle aren't you?"

CHAPTER TWENTY-SIX - DUEL

"Countess Blood?" asked Christiana.

"The very same," answered the vampire.

"Oh Lord preserve us from evil!" cried Gervase on seeing her.

"And who are you?" asked Bathory, her face returning to its human form.

"This is Father Gervase, he's had a bit of a rough time," replied Christiana as she helped the priest to limp out of the cell, the corridor was splashed scarlet and the thugs lay in contorted positions with their throats torn out. She felt a guilty satisfaction at seeing the groper's corpse there.

"So have you by the look of things?" remarked the vampire taking note of her bruises. "So this is the Watcher's fabled leader?"

"Yes creature, until you destroyed our church!" the priest had found some courage at last.

"Not my doing priest, spiker, take your Watcher and go down the manhole at the end of the corridor, it's a flood-drain and it'll take you out of here. You're on your own from then on!"

"No, Gervase can go alone, I'm staying. I have to find Thurlow."

"His real name is Gyorgy Thurzo who I, to my shame, created, what do you want with him?"

"He has information that will lead me to the creature that killed my parents," explained Van Helsing.

"He is my intended target also!"

"You must promise not to excise him until I have found out what I need."

"I will do my best spiker but I cannot make such a promise!" she noticed Gervase. "And why are you still here?" the priest scurried off in the direction Bathory indicated. "You will need weapons if you are to stay here and fight with me, Van Helsing."

"I had my holdall when they took me, if we can find it I will have all that I need!"

Bathory grunted non-committedly and strode towards the brightly-lit doorway at the end of the corridor with Christiana following. "What was this place used for?" she asked as they entered a square room tiled top to bottom in the same way as the "shower room".

There on a steel table in the centre was her sports bag, its contents spread out over the surface.

"It's an old asylum. Thurlow, as you know him, bought it last century and turned it into his lair. Fortunately for me when he renovated it he kept the cellars in their original state, this place is where uncooperative patients received *treatment*!" related Bathory as Christiana reacquainted herself with the tools of her ghastly trade.

"Someone's coming!" cried the spiker in alarm and the unlikely allies took up positions either side of the door.

As the vampire stepped into the room and before Bathory could stop her, Christina threw it against the wall, spiking it with expert ease to cause instant paralysis.

It was the nervous girl, Tamsin.

"Remove that spike immediately!" ordered Bathory.

"This is the creature Thurzo used to test my blood, it's one of them!"

"She's little more than a child and she's scared, release her or our truce is over."

Tina reluctantly pulled out the spike and Bathory caught her as she fell forward to say. "When you recover there's a way out of this hell at the end of the corridor and you'll find two fresh corpses there to help you heal, go now child and don't turn back."

Tina watched the girl stagger away with ill-concealed disgust. "Are you going to set free every vampire I spike?"

"We are people, not monsters, do you not understand that? You'll get your chance to quench your thirst for excision soon enough, Thurzo has plenty of thugs at his disposal but I warn you, some will be human. Can you kill one of your own kind so easily?"

Christiana did not reply but instead watched appalled as in the corridor, Tamsin, on her hands and knees, lapped at the open wound on the groper's throat.

"I thought not," said Bathory.

As they approached the stairs to the ground floor Bathory sniffed at the air then put up her hand and whispered. "There are two humans at the top of the stairs, stay here I will deal with them" she raced up the steps and the sound of fighting was followed by a body in fancy livery rolling limply down the stairs like a rag doll. "Come spiker!" called Bathory from above.

Upon crossing the long hall they were rushed by three of Thurzo's leather-jacketed vampire henchmen, Christiana hit one with a garlic bomb before spiking and decapitating it. Bathory beheaded a second with her parang then pushing the last against the wall, fired the nail gun repeatedly into its chest smiling as she recognised the face of the vampire whose eye she had put out then using her curved blade, inflicted the same fate upon it.

"Well fought ladies!" clapping came briefly from above. "Spiker, you fight so well it might be worth turning you after all and Erzsebet, it's such a delight to see you in action that I wish you had joined us!" Gyorgy Thurzo stood on the balcony flanked by vampires, some of whom were members of the Executive, he addressed the throng. "You see why I hold this woman in such great esteem? Erzsebet Bathory, I ask you one last time, will you join with us and help take back our rightful place in the world?"

"*Fattyu*, I will tear your heart out for what you have done!" she yelled, vampire and spiker now stood back to back as more of Thurzo's turnees emerged from doors around the hall.

"They've cut us off from the cellar steps," observed Christiana.

Bathory glanced around "They're blocking the front door too, the room to your right is our best chance, go for it and be careful with those bombs."

The mismatched pair achieved their goal taking down several assailants along the way, once inside Christiana threw several garlic bombs to keep the vampires at bay then helped Bathory to tip a large oak table up against the doors.

"Hey this is the dining room!" observed Christiana. "It's where Thurzo intended to serve me up for dinner."

Bathory was doubled up, the fumes from the garlic grenades making her retch. "This won't stand against them very long once they've regrouped" she affirmed and after regaining her composure crossed the room to throw back the long drapes. Behind them the windows were locked and shuttered against the daylight and barred into the bargain. "There's no way out, we are well and truly *szar*."

"Then we fight to the death!" cried Van Helsing defiantly.

"I fear we have little choice" affirmed Bathory.

A loud bang came against the barricaded door as Thurzo's men attempted to break through, there was a further crash and the doors moved slightly and after several more attempts the wood began to splinter. As the pair readied themselves for the inevitable something unexpected happened, the hammering on the doors ceased and sounds of combat came from without, then all fell quiet.

"Lizzie, are you alright in there?" a familiar voice broke the silence.

"Rob Roy?" asked Bathory.

"None other, John called me and suggested we come and help you. My boys were scouting around outside and they found a human priest ranting about a tunnel, don't worry yourself spiker, he's still alive and well. We also found a young one who told us all about Thurzo and his scheming."

"Have you got him?"

"That we have, now get this bloody door open." the pair moved the jammed table aside with some difficulty and ventured out into the hall, McGregor's clan were stationed around the room wearing police riot gear and armed with a variety of weapons. Some were standing guard over what was left of Thurzo's pack.

John Dee, who had accompanied them, scrutinised Christiana. "You are this fabled spiker I take it?"

"Yes and she is under my protection," stated Elisabeth firmly, some of Thurzo's guests on the balcony hissed their disapproval. "Now where is that *picsa*?"

"Elisabeth!" hissed Dee. "We only managed to win because we had the element of surprise, don't upset the others."

"Typical Erzsebet, putting the cattle before our people and this one here is the cow that kills!" shouted Thurzo who was being escorted down by a pair of McGregor's vampires.

"*Faszszopo geci!*" yelled Bathory changing to feral mode. "I'm going to tear you apart!"

McGregor seized her with some difficulty as she tried to rush Thurzo. "Lizzie, control yourself he's just trying to goad you."

"Think yourself lucky McGregor got to you before I did!" she growled.

"Better luck next time Erzsebet and how are your pets by the way, what are their names, James and Liz?" he sneered. "Oh, how the cow screamed when we bent her to fit that box."

Bathory howled in rage thrusting a claw-like hand towards him. "Let me go, McGregor!"

"Yes let her go Scotchman, this beast fucker does not frighten me."

"I challenge you Thurzo, before all those present, a fight to the excision!" she snarled.

"If I win the spiker is mine!" he replied.

She looked to the assembled notables on the balcony. "And if I win all of this stops?" most nodded acceptance.

"Hardly an even wager Erzsebet, but it is no matter, you will not survive to claim your prize," countered Thurzo.

"No weapons!" she snarled.

"As you wish Erzsebet!" agreed Thurzo, he was released and stretched out his fingers extending claw-like talons as his face elongated to a short bat-like muzzle. "No armour either." He pointed a claw at her stab-vest.

"Please Elisabeth, calm yourself, he will be tried and punished for his scheming." Dee insisted futilely as she shrugged off the body armour while McGregor held her tightly by the arm.

"Bathory, if you excise this creature I may never find who killed my parents!" cried Christiana.

Thurzo laughed. "So that is what you wanted spiker and you will go to your grave never knowing, will you beg for mercy as her pet did? I can still hear her bones cracking."

McGregor had loosened his grip on Bathory during the exchange and taking advantage of this she wrestled free to launch herself at Thurzo with a roar. "No, Elisabeth!"

he yelled fruitlessly.

Thurzo was ready and knocked her backwards then before she could recover he raked her side with razor-sharp claws tearing open her uniform to leave long deep gashes in her flesh. Bathory head-butted him in a very un-ladylike fashion then tore one side of his face open with her talons, the fight continued apace until both combatants were tiring and covered in dark red blood, neither seemed to have the upper hand until Thurzo got a blow through Bathory's guard hitting her hard on the chest and breaking several ribs in the process.

Bathory fell to her knees struggling for breath as her opponent moved in for the kill.

"Erzsebet my dam, you should have joined me, it gives me no real pleasure to do this." he swung his clawed hand back to take her head.

"*Baszd meg a szemét!*" Bathory snarled with dark red spittle foaming from her mouth and thrust a taloned hand into his stomach to push it up through the diaphragm into the ribcage then pulled it out her hand with something red and twitching clutched in it. "As I promised you Liz!" she yelled throwing Thurzo's heart into his astonished face. Staggering upright she took his head with a single swipe before his corpse sank to the floor then was caught gently in McGregor arms as she briefly lost consciousness.

Distraught, Christiana took up a defensive stance. She had lost the chance to find her parent's killer and was sur-rounded by vampires who would like nothing better than to tear her apart.

"It is over!" Dee roared to the assembly. "You will honour the Edict from now on, is that clear?" The group assembled on the balustrade muttered in agreement and began to disperse as Thurzo's remaining henchmen were led out in handcuffs. Dee then turned to Christiana. "Well, Miss Van Helsing, I will honour Elisabeth's pledge to keep you safe but what are we to do with you?"

Bathory had recovered slightly and gestured to him to

whisper something in his ear.

CHAPTER TWENTY-SEVEN
- PULASKI

"Hi I'm Constanza," said the girl with the riding crop.

Bedřich nodded approvingly taking in the athletic figure accentuated by the black leather corset with its spiked collar. Her blue eyes glittered behind a mask and long hair was tied in a high ponytail. "Where's Margaretta?" he asked curiously in an accent redolent of Bohemia.

"She's indisposed and I'm here in her place."

"Take off that mask and let me see your face Constanza," he ordered, the visage revealed was attractive in a girl-next-door sort of way and she seemed quite self-conscious. "You are very pretty but I think you are new to this, aren't you?"

"I'm no stranger to this sort of thing but this the first time I've done it like…"

He smiled revealing long teeth. "Do not trouble yourself, I am an old, old, man with much experience, look upon this as education," *she reminded him of someone.*

"Err…" she hesitated.

Bedřich laughing lightly and pleasantly said. "Come, come, dear girl, let us get to the business in hand and since I'm your first I'll pay you extra as an incentive" he eagerly undressed and the inexperienced dominatrix helped fasten his wrists and ankles into manacles attached to floor and ceiling. As she pressed close to finish restraining him he could feel the warmth of the blood in her veins and could see the pulse beating strongly her neck. Despite the spiky collar he had to resist the urge to bite, sinking his teeth into her jugular, *her blood must taste very sweet.*

"Is that alright?" she asked, this one reminded her of a kindly old grandfather and she actually felt some reluctance at going through with this. Hardening her resolve she thought, *just get it over and done with!*

She strutted around the chained captive on her spiked heels in what she hoped was an alluring manner while Bedřich looked her up and down appreciatively. "Well my dear, are we going to start?" he asked.

"If anything went wrong could you get out?" asked Constanza swishing the crop and holding it under his chin.

"Oh no I am completely helpless, that's the most pleasurable part of it, don't concern yourself, my dear I am no stranger to this," he liked this young woman, *I might turn her.*

"I am a bit puzzled, why does someone like you go in for this sort of thing?" she asked.

"Why are you surprised, is it because I am old, am I not allowed to indulge my pleasures?" He could feel both excitement and anxiety in the girl, finding it very arousing. He would turn her and she could serve him for eternity.

Her eyes widened as she noticed his state of excitement then stepping forward she swung the switch sideways across his cheek to slice it open.

"What was that for?" Bedřich demanded angrily, the crop had caused no permanent damage but it had stung considerably.

The leather-clad girl watched as the wound healed quickly and with very little bleeding. "Just making sure," she announced rummaging in a long bag on the floor next to the bench that was home to several interesting implements, then she advanced towards the man brandishing an iron spike in one hand and a cavalry sabre in the other.

"What would my poor dead mother think if she could see me like this, in stockings and leather with a naked man in chains?" she laughed sardonically. "Of course when I say man, I mean vampire!" she spat the last word as if had a bad taste.

Count Bedřich Pulaski raged and pulled at the chains with a strength and energy belying his elderly appearance. "And to think I was going to turn you!"

"As you did poor Margaretta?" the girl snapped. "I put her out of her misery before I came here."

"Who are you?" the vampire snarled.

"I am Christiana Van Helsing and as I told you, I am no stranger to this, but admittedly it is the first time I've worn a bondage outfit to do it!" she held the point of the spike to his ribcage. "Any last words Count?"

"You're Ilse Van Helsing's daughter!" he cried in shocked realisation.

A police escort had been arranged to take Christiana to Gatwick (to make certain she left) and before going through security the young constable had pressed a written note from Elisabeth into her hand, it contained Pulaski's full name and the address of the S&M dungeons he frequented.

"You've got it in one you undead bastard!" she cried and teeth bared drove the spike in hard then stood back and watched the vampire sag forward. Changing the sabre to her right hand, Christiana swung at the scrawny neck. "This is for you *Moeder*!"

The End

Other titles by **BLKDOG** Publishing that
you may enjoy:

Sirkkusaga
By Kyt Wright

A saga – a long story of heroic achievement, especially a medieval prose narrative in Old Norse or a long, involved story, account, or series of incidents often named for the principal character.

Several hundred years after an world-shattering war, two of the surviving nations, the Reignweald and the Dominion have fought themselves to a standstill, both remaining determined to control of what's left of it.

Sirki Vigsdottir, a songstress who performs under the name Freya in folk-rock group *The Harvest* is beautiful, self-centered woman who is fond of drink and a recovering addict to boot, not the sort of girl a boy brings home to mother.

Following an attack from an unexpected quarter, abilities awaken within Sirki, who begins a journey of self-discovery. These new found skills attract the attention of both the Psi, a mysterious group of telepaths headed by the fearsome Mina and an equally sinister government department; the ACG.

Sirki, learning the real truth of her origin, is dragged into plotting between the queen and the Government, finding herself in constant danger as Bren, fighting for the nation, becomes an important part of her life.As it becomes clear that her life of self-indulgence is over, Sirki wonders if her new-found powers are a blessing or a curse.

Arthur: Shadow of a God
By Richard Denham

King Arthur has fascinated the Western world for over a thousand years and yet we still know nothing more about him now than we did then. Layer upon layer of heroics and exploits has been piled upon him to the point where history, legend and myth have become hopelessly entangled.

In recent years, there has been a sort of scholarly consensus that 'the once and future king' was clearly some sort of Romano-British warlord, heroically stemming the tide of wave after wave of Saxon invaders after the end of Roman rule. But surprisingly, and no matter how much we enjoy this narrative, there is actually next-to-nothing solid to support this theory except the wishful thinking of understandably bitter contemporaries. The sources and scholarship used to support the 'real Arthur' are as much tentative guesswork and pushing 'evidence' to the extreme to fit in with this version as anything involving magic swords, wizards and dragons. Even Archaeology remains silent. Arthur is, and always has been, the square peg that refuses to fit neatly into the historians round hole.

Arthur: Shadow of a God gives a fascinating overview of Britain's lost hero and casts a light over an often-overlooked and somewhat inconvenient truth; Arthur was almost certainly not a man at all, but a god. He is linked inextricably to the world of Celtic folklore and Druidic traditions. Whereas tyrants like Nero and Caligula were men who fancied themselves gods; is it not possible that Arthur was a god we have turned into a man? Perhaps then there is a truth here. Arthur, 'The King under the Mountain'; sleeping until his return will never return, after all, because he doesn't need to. Arthur the god never left in the first place and remains as popular today as he ever was. His legend echoes in stories, films and games that are every bit as imaginative and fanciful as that which the minds of talented bards such as Taliesin and Aneirin came up with when the mists of the 'dark ages' still swirled over Britain – and perhaps that is a good thing after all, most at home in the imaginations of children and adults alike – being the Arthur his believers want him to be.

A Storm of Magic
By Ashley Laino

Being brought back from the dead is an impressive trick, even for magician Darien Burron. Now he must try and use his sleight of hand to swindle modern-day witch, Mirah, to sign her power away, or end up a tormented demon in the afterlife.

Meanwhile, sixteen-year-old Mirah is starting to lose control of her powers. After an incident at her aunt's Witchery store, Mirah is sent to a secret coven to learn to control her abilities. While away, Mirah meets up with a soft-spoken clairvoyant, a brazen storm witch, and the creator of dark magic itself. The young woman must learn to trust in herself before she loses herself entirely to the darkness that hunts her.

Weirder War Two
By Richard Denham & Michael Jecks

Did a Warner Bros. cartoon prophesize the use of the atom bomb? Did the Allies really plan to use stink bombs on the enemy? Why did the Nazis make their own version of Titanic and why were polar bear photographs appearing throughout Europe?

The Second World War was the bloodiest of all wars. Mass armies of men trudged, flew or rode from battlefields as far away as North Africa to central Europe, from India to Burma, from the Philippines to the borders of Japan. It saw the first aircraft carrier sea battle, and the indiscriminate use of terror against civilian populations in ways not seen since the Thirty Years War. Nuclear and incendiary bombs erased entire cities. V weapons brought new horror from the skies: the V1 with their hideous grumbling engines, the V2 with sudden, unexpected death. People were systematically starved: in Britain food had to be rationed because of the stranglehold of U-Boats, while in Holland the German blockage of food and fuel saw 30,000 die of starvation in the winter of 1944/5. It was a catastrophe for millions.

At a time of such enormous crisis, scientists sought ever more inventive weapons, or devices to help halt the war. Civilians were involved as never before, with women taking up new trades, proving themselves as capable as their male predecessors whether in the factories or the fields.

The stories in this book are of courage, of ingenuity, of hilarity in some cases, or of great sadness, but they are all thought-provoking - and rather weird. So whether you are interested in the last Polish cavalry charge, the Blackout Ripper, Dada, or Ghandi's attempt to stop the bloodshed, welcome to the Weirder War Two!

Click Bait
By Gillian Philip

A funny joke's a funny joke. Eddie Doolan doesn't think twice about adapting it to fit a tragic local news story and posting it on social media.

It's less of a joke when his drunken post goes viral. It stops being funny altogether when Eddie ends up jobless, friendless and ostracized by the whole town of Langburn. This isn't how he wanted to achieve fame.

Under siege from the press, and facing charges not just for the joke but for a history of abusive behavior on the internet, Eddie grows increasingly paranoid and desperate. The only people still speaking to him are Crow, a neglected kid who relies on Eddie for food and company, and Sid, the local gamekeeper's granddaughter. It's Sid who offers Eddie a refuge and an understanding ear.

But she also offers him an illegal shotgun - and as Eddie's life spirals downwards, and his efforts at redemption are thwarted at every turn, the gun starts to look like the answer to all his problems.

Burning Bridges
By Chris Bedell

They've always said that three's a crowd...

24-year-old Sasha didn't anticipate her identical twin Riley killing herself upon their reconciliation after years of estrangement. But Sasha senses an opportunity and assumes Riley's identity so she can escape her old life.

Playing Riley isn't without complications, though. Riley's had a strained relationship with her wife and stepson so Sasha must do whatever she can to make her newfound family love and accept her. If Sasha's arrangement ends, then she'll have nothing protecting her from her past. However, when one of Sasha's former clients tracks her down, Sasha must choose between her new life and the only person who cared about her.

But things are about to become even more complicated, as a third sister, Katrina, enters the scene...

**Father of Storms
By Dean Jones**

Imagine losing everything you loved as well as the future you'd wished for so long to come true.

Seth was born with the gift to manipulate energy, unfortunately his skills mark him as a target for one who wishes to control everything. So began a life running from those who would seek to command him, a life that spans over a thousand years waiting for the day when all will be once again as it was.

Captured in modern day London, Seth needs the help of his companions, the Mara, to show him who he is through dreams of his past, so he can save the family he has waited so long to have. A warrior bred for battle must fight once more but this time the battlefield is his mind. Can Seth win, or will he finally lose who he is and become the weapon of the man who started his nightmare all those years ago? *Father of Storms* is a story told through time, a tale of love and hope where there seems to be none and above all it is a reminder that if you believe, truly believe then even from the darkest places, good things come to those who wait.

www.blkdogpublishing.com